FROM THE
NANCY DREW FILES

THE CASE: *Nancy investigates a series of thefts at the trendy Vanities boutique and finds that murder is all the rage.*

CONTACT: *Nancy's next-door neighbor, Nikki Masters, fell in love with the wrong guy, Dan Taylor. When the romance dies, so does Dan. Now Nancy's the only one who can prove Nikki's innocence.*

SUSPECTS: *Trisha Rapp—the manager of Vanities. She has the brains and the ambition to move on to bigger and better places—and she'll stop at nothing to get there.*

Max Hudson—the body-building stockboy. Everyone knows he always hated Dan, and no one knows where he was when Dan died.

Tony Selby—the salesman with a shady past, a red-hot temper, and a girlfriend he just might kill for.

COMPLICATIONS: *Nikki Masters has Nancy on her side, but the police have the evidence on theirs: they found Nikki's purse at the scene of the crime.*

Books in THE NANCY DREW FILES® Series

#1 SECRETS CAN KILL
#2 DEADLY INTENT
#3 MURDER ON ICE
#4 SMILE AND SAY MURDER
#5 HIT AND RUN HOLIDAY
#6 WHITE WATER TERROR
#7 DEADLY DOUBLES
#8 TWO POINTS TO MURDER
#9 FALSE MOVES
#10 BURIED SECRETS
#11 HEART OF DANGER
#12 FATAL RANSOM
#13 WINGS OF FEAR
#14 THIS SIDE OF EVIL
#15 TRIAL BY FIRE
#16 NEVER SAY DIE
#17 STAY TUNED FOR DANGER
#18 CIRCLE OF EVIL
#19 SISTERS IN CRIME

#20 VERY DEADLY YOURS
#21 RECIPE FOR MURDER
#22 FATAL ATTRACTION
#23 SINISTER PARADISE
#24 TILL DEATH DO US PART
#25 RICH AND DANGEROUS
#26 PLAYING WITH FIRE
#27 MOST LIKELY TO DIE
#28 THE BLACK WIDOW
#29 PURE POISON
#30 DEATH BY DESIGN
#31 TROUBLE IN TAHITI
#32 HIGH MARKS FOR MALICE
#33 DANGER IN DISGUISE
#34 VANISHING ACT
#35 BAD MEDICINE
#36 OVER THE EDGE
#37 LAST DANCE
#38 THE FINAL SCENE
#39 THE SUSPECT NEXT DOOR

Available from ARCHWAY paperbacks

THE
NANCY DREW
FILES™ CASE • 39

THE SUSPECT
NEXT DOOR

Carolyn Keene

AN ARCHWAY PAPERBACK
Published by POCKET BOOKS
New York   London   Toronto   Sydney   Tokyo

AN ARCHWAY PAPERBACK *Original*

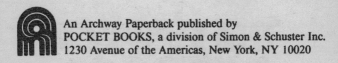

An Archway Paperback published by
POCKET BOOKS, a division of Simon & Schuster Inc.
1230 Avenue of the Americas, New York, NY 10020

ISBN: 0-671-67491-9

First Archway Paperback printing September 1989

10 9 8 7 6 5 4 3 2 1

NANCY DREW, AN ARCHWAY PAPERBACK and colophon
are registered trademarks of Simon & Schuster Inc.

THE NANCY DREW FILES is a trademark
of Simon & Schuster Inc.

Printed in the U.S.A.

IL 7+

THE SUSPECT NEXT DOOR

Chapter

One

I'M CRAZY ABOUT YOU, NAN."

Nancy Drew's eyes were still shut after Ned's long, lingering kiss. She felt his breath on her ear as he uttered those magic words. A ripple of delight slid up her spine.

Opening her eyes, Nancy gazed into the warm, handsome face of her boyfriend, Ned Nickerson. Behind him, the setting sun shone through the dappled leaves of the trees in the park.

"You know something?" Nancy said with a glowing smile.

"Hmmm?" Ned murmured.

"I've got to be the luckiest girl in the entire universe. You're a wonderful guy, Ned Nickerson." Brushing a strand of reddish blond hair from her face, she leaned against him and reached down to hold his hand.

"The feeling is totally mutual," Ned said, nuzzling her neck.

Resting her head on Ned's strong, muscular shoulder, Nancy thought back over the last few weeks. Summer had been fabulous.

If only their time together could last forever. If only summer didn't have to end.

In less than a week Ned would be going back to Emerson College. That meant nine long months of seeing him only on holidays and an occasional weekend.

Nancy sighed and snuggled closer to Ned. Her hip brushed up against her purse, and she felt the portable radio she'd bought for Ned earlier that day. It was her anniversary present for him, and she could hardly wait to give it to him.

She couldn't help wondering, though, if he had remembered it was their anniversary. Oh, don't be silly, she told herself. Of course he did.

"What are you thinking?" he asked, nuzzling her ear.

Nancy gazed up at him through the gathering darkness and ran a hand through his wavy brown hair. She was trying to fix his image in her memory. "I was thinking I'm going to miss you terribly."

Across the brook, on the path that led down to
the big weeping willow trees and the riverfront,
Nancy caught sight of a young couple strolling,
hand in hand, their heads together, deep in
conversation.

Nancy recognized the girl immediately. It was
her neighbor, Nikki Masters. Just sixteen, Nikki
was a slender, blue-eyed blonde with a sweet,
gentle nature. Nancy didn't recognize the guy,
who was about Ned's age. He was wearing a
jacket with a gold eagle patch on the arm.

"Look, Ned," she whispered. "Over there.
Aren't they cute?"

"Mmmm." Ned nodded and tossed an arm
over her shoulder. A slow grin came over his face.
"Reminds me of us."

Nancy giggled. "Don't you recognize her?
That's Nikki, my next-door neighbor."

"That's Nikki? Wow!" said Ned with surprise.
"She sure has grown up. Who's the guy she's
with?"

"I don't know. But I think this is her first big
romance."

Ned clasped Nancy's shoulder a little tighter
and gave it a quick squeeze. "And you're mine,
Nancy. My first, last, and only."

Nancy bit her lip and felt a blush spread over
her cheeks. She had met other guys who turned
her head temporarily. But she'd always been
loyal to Ned.

Turning toward him, she tenderly ran her fingertips over his strong jaw. "I love you, too, Ned, only you. Now and always," she murmured.

Before she knew it, their lips were meeting in another sizzling kiss. A bolt of glorious electricity went straight through Nancy.

Slipping out of Ned's embrace, she took one last look across the park. Nikki and her friend were leaving.

As Nancy watched, Nikki yanked her hand from her boyfriend's and started walking away from him. Despite the boy's pleas, Nikki refused to turn around. Instead she ran to the parking lot, got in her car and drove off—leaving her boyfriend standing alone by his dented blue car.

That's strange, Nancy thought. But then, first romances weren't always easy. Not everyone was as lucky as she and Ned.

"He's just so thoughtful. So sweet." Nancy couldn't stop bragging about Ned the next afternoon. She and her best friends, Bess Marvin and George Fayne, were on a shopping excursion at River Heights Mall.

"You are *soooo* lucky!" Bess pulled on a strand of her blond hair in mock frustration. "If only they could clone Ned. Why, oh why, are all the good ones taken?"

"Come on, Bess," Nancy teased. "It's been a grand total of three weeks since you've been madly in love."

4

"Three weeks? Try two days." Bess's first cousin, George Fayne, rolled her eyes. Despite her name, George was definitely a girl—tall, lean, and athletic, with short curly dark hair and intelligent brown eyes. "You've got to admit it, Bess. You're just not a one-man woman," she added.

Bess's mouth took on a pretty pout, and she put her hands on her hips. "How can you say that! I am, too!" she insisted. "It's just that I haven't found the right 'one man' yet!"

That sent all three girls off on a fit of laughter. The only thing better than a good friend is *two* good friends, Nancy reflected. Bess and George were even a big help when it came to her detective work.

"All I can say is, thank goodness for shopping," Bess said with a sigh. "It alone makes this lonely life worthwhile. Hey, check out that dress. Can't you just see me in that?"

Bess's sparkling blue eyes were fixed on a fiery red dress in the window of Vanities, the mall's most exclusive boutique. The dress had an off-the-shoulder top, decorated with black sequins; the skirt was made of the sleekest scarlet satin. A red bolero jacket with black satin piping completed the outfit.

"It's beautiful," George said, her eyes wide. "And just think, all you'd need is a few hundred dollars and you could actually buy it!"

Bess sighed. "A few hundred dollars and a

two-month diet." Bess was forever trying to lose weight, even though her figure was only five pounds heavier than perfect.

Nancy and George gave each other a look. Bess was staring at the dress, unable to move. "I have a feeling my hips would look really svelte in that dress," she murmured.

"You want to try it on, don't you?" George asked sympathetically.

"Okay, let's go in," Nancy agreed. "But, George, you've got to promise to help me sew up Bess's broken heart after she reads the price tag. Okay?"

"Sure," George said cheerfully as she pushed the glass door open for her friends. "I'm an expert at that by now."

As the three girls walked into the shop, they were immediately overwhelmed. Clothes were just a part of Vanities. The store featured accessories, too: belts, bags, and exclusive designer jewelry. Many of the items were one of a kind, and the prices ranged from expensive to out of this world.

There were dressed mannequins and display cases artfully placed to lead the shopper farther and farther into the store. Right in front, where Nancy was standing, was the cashier's station. The cashier was an attractive girl with oversize glasses, pale skin, and curly dark hair cut shoulder length.

At the moment, she was being lectured by an elegantly dressed middle-aged woman with steel gray eyes and well-styled, upswept black hair.

"This is not an ordinary store," the woman was saying. "You've got to learn to project more confidence. Vanities has a certain image, one that I have worked hard to establish. You're going to have to do more to project that image."

The older woman wore a close-cut conservative suit, not of the type that was featured at Vanities, but her oversize silver and lapis earrings gave her great style.

From the way the cashier listened to her, Nancy guessed the woman must be the owner of Vanities.

"Oh, look! Aren't these adorable!" Hearing Bess call her, Nancy turned and saw her holding two red-feathered earrings up to the sides of her head. "They'd go perfectly with that dress in the window."

Bess rushed over to the girl behind the register. "I've got to try on that incredible red dress in the window," she confessed. "Do you have it in size seven?"

"I'm not sure, but I guess I can check," the girl said timidly.

"Oh, I love jade," George cooed as she hovered over a display case filled with beautiful green ornaments and jewelry.

"And look here!" Bess cried excitedly. "Check

7

out this jewelry! It's so great. Nancy, that blue necklace would look terrific on you."

The display case Bess was looking at contained jewelry made of silver, turquoise, and acrylic. It was the most unusual jewelry Nancy had ever seen.

"It's super!" George agreed. "And Bess is right about that blue one, Nan. It matches your eyes perfectly."

The older woman saw them looking at the jewelry, walked over, and silently lifted the tray out of the case.

"Thanks," Nancy said, reaching for the necklace her friends had pointed to. On the back was an inscribed *Z*, which looked like a bolt of lightning. Nancy guessed it was probably the jeweler's mark.

Nancy flipped the price tag over. The necklace cost sixty-five dollars. Nancy had enough money from her birthday to buy the necklace, but she decided to wait. She was hoping Ned might surprise her with a piece of jewelry for their anniversary. Wearing things he picked out for her was a lot more fun than buying them for herself.

"It's lovely," Nancy said, placing the necklace back on the tray.

The curly-haired salesgirl came over to them. "Sorry," she told Bess regretfully. "We're out of that dress."

Bess's face fell, and her eyes went to the dress in the window. "What about that one?"

The girl shook her head. "I think it's a size three," she said tentatively.

"Excuse me, Charlene." The owner approached them. "We just got that shipment in yesterday. Did you check in the stockroom?"

"Yes, Ms. Hayes." The salesgirl was completely flustered. "There are none left. I looked everywhere."

"You must have missed them, Charlene," Ms. Hayes said with a worried smile. "I'll check myself."

She strode to the back of the store and disappeared into the stockroom. The three girls stood there, a little embarrassed for the salesgirl.

A few moments later Ms. Hayes reemerged. "Trisha!" she called out in a loud voice.

A pretty girl of about twenty-five with a clipboard under her arm ran over from across the shop. She had ear-length ash blond hair held up on one side with a large green barrette. "What is it, Ms. Hayes?"

"The red bolero outfit in the window? Didn't it come in just yesterday?"

"Yes. A dozen of them, in sizes five to thirteen. See here?" She pointed to a notation on a form attached to the clipboard. Nancy edged closer.

"And how many were sold?" Ms. Hayes asked, a look of confusion clouding over her eyes.

Trisha bit her lip and checked farther down on the page. "None yet," she said weakly.

9

"You know what that means, don't you?" Ms. Hayes asked. Nancy noticed there was an edge to her voice.

Trisha was silent. Ms. Hayes answered for her. "It means Vanities has been robbed again!"

Chapter

Two

NANCY WATCHED as the owner of Vanities marched to the phone and dialed what she knew was the number for the police. Trisha slipped her clipboard behind the cash register and busied herself with a waiting customer.

Charlene Rice, the salesgirl-cashier, gave Nancy and her friends a helpless shrug. "Sorry about all this," she began awkwardly. "We've been having a few problems around here lately."

When the store owner hung up the phone, Nancy approached her. "Excuse me," she began. "My name's Nancy Drew. These are my friends, George Fayne and Bess Marv—"

"Nancy Drew!" the owner interrupted, her

eyes widening. "The detective? Yes, now that I look at you, I do recognize you from the newspapers. I'm Kate Hayes," she added, offering her hand to Nancy. "I'm the owner of this store."

"If there's any way I can help, Ms. Hayes, I'd be happy to."

Ms. Hayes seemed surprised. "You really mean that?" she asked. When Nancy nodded, she went on. "Because I've called the police in every time this has happened, and they keep telling me there's not much they can do. There's never any sign of a forced entry; nothing shows up on the film from the security cameras. They say it's obviously an inside job and tell me to keep an eye on my staff!"

Ms. Hayes gestured around her. The store was busy, with about a dozen customers being waited on. Looking back at Nancy, Ms. Hayes said, "I'm a businesswoman. I can't stand around here spying on my own employees. It's impossible. I have two other stores to look after. I can't just fire everybody, either. That would mean hurting a lot of innocent people. I just don't know where to turn! This theft is the fourth in just six weeks, and—"

"Ms. Hayes," Nancy broke in.

"Please, call me Kate."

"All right, then, Kate. I think we should continue this conversation in private—considering the circumstances." Nancy held up a hand and exchanged a knowing look with Bess and George.

Kate Hayes looked around again, more warily this time. "Mmmm, I suppose you're right. Trisha!"

Trisha immediately excused herself from her customer and hurried over to Ms. Hayes's side.

"Trisha Rapp, this is Nancy Drew. Trisha's our store manager, Nancy, and a very good one, too. She's the one who first brought the thefts to my attention. Trisha will be able to give you any facts and figures you need."

Trisha glanced at Nancy, then at her employer. "I don't understand," she said. "Is she a police officer?"

"Trisha, Nancy is a well-known detective here in River Heights. I've asked her to help us investigate our theft problem and put an end to this nonsense before it puts an end to Vanities."

"I see." Trisha chewed her lip thoughtfully.

"We need all the help we can get around here," Ms. Hayes added with a shake of her head. "Oh!" she continued, "these are Nancy's friends, er—"

"Bess Marvin."

"George Fayne." The two girls gave identical nods.

"Bess and George," Ms. Hayes finished. Then she turned to Nancy. "Trisha's new to River Heights, Nancy. What's it been, Trisha, six months?" Trisha nodded. "So you'll forgive her if she's never heard of you."

Nancy laughed, holding out her hand to Trisha.

THE NANCY DREW FILES

"I'm looking forward to working with you. Maybe together we'll get to the bottom of all this."

"Yes. That would be nice." Trisha shook Nancy's hand but seemed distracted. "Are the police coming?" Trisha asked her employer.

"Oh, I almost forgot," Ms. Hayes moaned, "they'll be here any minute. We'd better close early tonight, Trisha. We can't have customers here with the police."

Kate Hayes seemed distinctly frustrated. "I'd better get on the phone to report this to my insurance company, too. I may have a hard time trying to convince them not to cancel our policy," she said. "Can you girls handle the police if they show up while I'm still on the phone?"

"Sure thing, Ms. Hayes." Trisha nodded.

Nancy checked her watch. It was five o'clock, and she was supposed to meet Ned at a quarter to six. Oh, well. She'd been late before. Thank goodness Ned was so understanding.

"You're so bubbly tonight, Nan," Ned said, gazing into her eyes as they stood on the sidewalk, pulling on their jackets. "There's a special gleam in your eyes. Was it the movie, or is it just being with me?"

"Actually, it's neither," Nancy said, laughing. "I'm on a new case."

Ned's eyes widened, and he drew in a deep breath. "Oh, so that's it!" he said brightly. "Well,

I suppose that's better than your being in love with someone else."

"One guy is enough for me," Nancy said sweetly. She knew Ned was joking to cover his concern for her safety. Lots of times, her cases were dangerous. She knew Ned worried about her when he was away at school, unable to help. And here he was, leaving next week just as a new case was beginning.

"It's just some store thefts, Ned. Nothing heavy. I'm going to try to wind it up this week. In fact, so we could have more time together, I could use some help—"

"Did I hear you say 'help'? Sergeant Nickerson of the Yukon at your service, ma'am!" He paused to salute. "When do I start?"

"I'll let you know," Nancy answered. "But it's nice to know my Mountie is still available."

"Which store is it?" Ned asked as they headed for his car.

"A store in the mall called Vanities," she answered. "They've been robbed several times in the past month and a half. The police seem reluctant to get involved."

"Oh? Why's that?"

"Well, it looks like an inside job. No sign of a break-in—somebody knows all about the store's security. Maybe the police figure it's a scam of some kind. At any rate, so far they've left it up to the insurance company."

Ned reached around Nancy's waist as they continued down the street.

"Sounds pretty tame, actually," Ned said, trying to look hopeful. "How are you going to proceed?"

"Tomorrow morning I'll go over all the store's records and interview the employees. Nothing earth-shattering." Nancy smiled up at him. "I can handle that by myself, but if I need you—"

"I'm all yours." Ned hugged her close to him.

The street was dark now, and many of the shops were closed for the night. Ned's car was parked at the near corner. Ned turned to Nancy and asked, "Want to go for pizza? Old movies make me hungry."

"You bet," Nancy smiled. "Frank's is open. Why don't we walk? It's only two blocks."

Turning the corner, they strolled down to the popular teen hangout. The sound of a current top-ten hit filtered out of the restaurant and into the street. Even though it was past ten-thirty, the place was still hopping. In fact, every seat was taken.

"What do you say we just get a couple of slices to go and eat them on my porch?" Nancy suggested softly.

"Fine with me," he replied, kissing the side of her head. "Sounds kind of romantic, actually. Pizza on the Porch for Two." With a wink at Nancy, he turned and placed their order.

* * *

Nancy and Ned set up their late-night picnic on a wicker table on Nancy's front porch.

"Pizza, a full moon, and you," Ned said, and sighed. "I love it. Come here and sit down," he said, patting the spot next to him on the love seat.

"Last time we spent an evening on the porch, we were up talking till two in the morning," she recalled.

"Not just talking," Ned reminded her, kissing her tenderly on her lips.

"Mmmm," Nancy breathed. "You Royal Mounted Police are all so romantic. And you also know how to make a girl hungry. Where's the pizza? I'm starving."

"Hey, I was just getting started over here!" Ned said, holding out her slice and a napkin. "Do you mean to say pizza is more important to you than me?"

"A girl's got to eat," Nancy said with a shrug and a laugh. "Besides, there's nothing like food to make a person feel romantic."

"Is that so?" said Ned, arching his eyebrows. "Well, then." Brushing his hands together, he reached for his slice. "Let me at it." Ned folded his pizza wedge, winked at Nancy, and took a big bite.

As they ate Nancy watched a beat-up old car stop in front of the house next door. Nancy recognized Nikki Masters and her boyfriend as they got out of the car. "Remember those two from the park?" Nancy whispered to Ned, throwing him a knowing look.

Ned nodded. He and Nancy munched quietly, watching the young couple as they strolled up to the Masterses' house and said their good-nights. The boy had his arm around Nikki, and he leaned his head very close to hers.

"Love springs eternal," Ned said in a soft whisper.

Nancy was about to answer when, suddenly, Nikki wrenched free from her boyfriend's grasp and ran up on the porch.

"I told you, no!" Nikki said forcefully.

"Nikki! Wait!" the boy shouted, following her. He caught up to her and grabbed her wrist. Nancy and Ned couldn't help hearing what they were saying.

"Please!" the boy said. "Please take it!"

"I told you I can't!" Nancy could tell that Nikki was really upset.

"But you've got to take it!" the boy insisted. "Please."

Nancy and Ned were embarrassed to be in on such a private moment. But there was really nowhere they could go without making the couple aware of their presence, and they didn't want to interrupt.

"Let me go! Please!" Nikki cried suddenly, pulling her hand out of the boy's grasp. Ned had moved as if he were going to Nikki's rescue, but Nancy put a hand on his knee to restrain him.

Nancy didn't feel right about nosing in on her neighbor's business—unless Nikki needed help.

The boy had let his arms drop to his sides. "Don't you care if I live or die?" he demanded. "I'm telling you, Nikki, I can't make it without you! Please."

"Oh, stop it! Stop it!" Nikki pleaded. "Dan, please! Leave me alone! I can't stand it anymore! I wish you the best, I really do. But I just don't want all this trouble." Nikki ran for the door.

This time Dan didn't try to stop her. Instead, he shook his head and stared at the ground. "You don't understand, Nikki."

"I guess I don't, Dan. I'm sorry, I r-really am," Nikki stammered, turning to face him. "But I just can't handle all your problems."

Dan's eyes opened wide. In the light of the Masterses' porch, he looked more afraid than angry, but when he spoke, the anger was definitely there. "Why don't you just admit it? You don't care! You wouldn't even care if I died!"

Nancy knew Nikki's face must be reddening. "Stop trying to make me feel guilty, Dan Taylor! Leave me alone!" she said firmly and coldly. "If you don't I just might kill you myself!"

Chapter

Three

Nikki slammed the door behind her as Dan Taylor skulked back to his car and drove off. Exchanging a look, Nancy and Ned put down their half-eaten slices of pizza and breathed out loud.

"Whew." Ned sighed. "What do you suppose that was all about?"

Nancy thought for a second. "I don't know, Ned," she admitted, "but those two seem to have some serious problems. Do you think I should—"

"Do I think you should get involved?" Ned finished for her. "Absolutely not."

"But Nikki's my neighbor, Ned. I've known

her for a long time. She's always been so levelheaded and sure of herself. I've never seen her upset like that."

"Come on, Nan," Ned said with a sigh. "It's young love. First-time romances are always stormy."

"I don't know." Nancy didn't feel right about it. She knew Ned was probably right. Some young couples had fights every day. She and Ned had had a few spats during the first months they were together.

But the exchange Nancy had overheard didn't sound like a simple spat. Nancy couldn't help worrying about Nikki. Something was really upsetting her. Maybe if Nikki had a shoulder to cry on, someone to talk to . . .

Nancy knew Nikki wasn't prone to threatening people. Still, Nikki had *sounded* as if she *meant* it. Nancy decided that the next time she saw Nikki she'd find out if there was anything she could do to help her.

Kate Hayes was waiting anxiously when Nancy got to Vanities the next morning. "I've got to take care of things in my two other stores," she explained quickly. "Fortunately, there haven't been any thefts there. Here's a list of my employees," she said, handing Nancy a piece of yellow legal paper. "I'll check in with you later. Meanwhile, Trisha will help you out."

Trisha nodded her assent. "Right, Ms. Hayes.

Don't worry. I'll handle things here. And I'm sure Ms. Drew will hold up her end."

"Please call me Nancy," Nancy corrected her when Kate Hayes had gone.

"Sure," Trisha said, barely managing a smile. "Well, what do you want to start with? I've got a lot of work to do back in the stockroom, so—"

Nancy noticed that the minute Kate Hayes left the store, Trisha's eager attitude dropped away. "If you don't mind, I'll just tag along with you, to get a feel for the place," Nancy said.

"That's up to you," Trisha said with a shrug, leading her back through the door to the stockroom.

"What kind of security system do you have here?" Nancy asked.

"Oh, Vanities is well-protected," Trisha answered, pointing to electronic devices spaced along the walls up near the ceiling. "We have a supersophisticated alarm system, complete with video cameras. There are magnetic tags on most of the merchandise and electronic locks with codes on the front door and the door to the loading area in back."

"Then it would be pretty hard to break into from the outside," Nancy murmured. "How many hours a week is Ms. Hayes here?"

"About three hours a day, on the average. Except when she's on a buying trip. Then she can be gone for up to two weeks at a time."

So there really was no efficient way of preventing an inside job, Nancy thought as they made their way past racks of clothing.

She wondered if there was a way of keeping track of when each employee was in the store. "Are the people who work here on a set schedule?" she asked.

"Not really. There is a schedule, but it's always being changed. Most of the sales help is part-time. There's no logging-in system on the registers, or anything like that. Ms. Hayes mostly leaves us alone to get our work done."

Nancy realized that meant it would be relatively easy for anyone who worked there to tamper with the camera system and sneak merchandise out the back way to the loading dock.

"Who knows the electronic code on the doors?" she asked.

"Just Ms. Hayes," Trisha answered. "And me, of course. One of us is always here to open the store. But the codes are changed weekly."

From the police the day before, Nancy knew that the amount of merchandise stolen was large. Too much for one person to smuggle out during working hours. Someone must have found out how to open the coded locks, disarm the security system, and rob the store while it was closed.

"Is there somewhere private for me to interview the rest of the staff?" Nancy asked when they stepped into Trisha's small inner office.

"Sure," Trisha answered. "You can use my office." Although she was being cooperative,

Trisha's manner had not warmed up. She went to her desk and took out a few sheets of paper. "I'd better go up front and open the cash register. We really don't have that many people working here. I'll start sending them in right away."

In the brief time Nancy was alone, she checked out Trisha's office. On the desk were inventory sheets and employee records. In the top drawer was a huge account ledger. Everything relevant to the store's business was probably in this office. Nancy would have to go through it all later.

She wondered about Trisha. After all, who in the store was in a better position to carry out a series of thefts? But if Trisha was behind it all, why would she have blown the whistle? The thefts might have gone undetected for a long time, but she had called them to Kate Hayes's attention instead.

Nancy heard a knock on the door. Charlene Rice was standing in the doorway, looking nervous. "Trisha said you wanted to see me. I really don't know anything. I didn't even know there'd been any robberies until Trisha told me." The words spilled out of Charlene. From the way she looked at Nancy, it was as if she thought she were about to be sentenced.

"Well, come on in, anyway. There's a lot I need to know about the store and how it operates," Nancy said with a friendly smile.

Charlene stepped into the little room. To Nancy's surprise, a large man with bushy dark eyebrows and a thick crop of wavy black hair came in after her. Nancy recognized him as another employee.

"This is Tony. Tony Selby," Charlene explained. "He's a salesman for the men's clothing line we've just added."

"Hi, Tony," Nancy greeted him. "I'm looking forward to meeting everyone on staff. Would you mind waiting until I've talked to Charlene?"

Tony didn't move. "It's okay," he stated flatly. "If you got a question for Charlene, you can ask her in front of me."

"Tony's my boyfriend," Charlene explained in a trembling voice. "He's just trying to protect me."

"Oh?" Nancy's eyebrows jumped up. "Is there something in particular you need protection from?"

Tony tensed, but Charlene put a hand on his arm and said, "Well, I was kind of in the middle of it yesterday, when the dresses were found missing."

"Listen! If you think Charlene took those dresses, you're nuts," Tony put in. "And I didn't steal them, either. So go ahead and ask your questions, okay?"

"Sure." Nancy cleared her throat. "Well, you two know a lot more about Vanities than I do. Who do you think is stealing from the store? Any ideas?"

Charlene bit her lip nervously, shook her head,

and studied the toes of her shoes. Tony stood there glaring at Nancy. A silence descended over the office. Nancy was determined not to be the first to break it.

"I have an idea all right," Tony finally told Nancy. "You ever hear of an insurance scam? That's what I think is going on. I think she's saying these things are gone so she can collect for them." Tony looked proud of his theory.

"You mean Kate Hayes, of course," Nancy asked.

Tony nodded. "That happens a lot, you know."

Charlene put her hand on Tony's arm to quiet him. "You won't repeat any of this to Ms. Hayes, will you, Ms. Drew? Tony's just a little upset because of the way Ms. Hayes treated me. But I understand. She's been under a lot of stress lately."

"I won't say anything," Nancy said, her eyes moving from Charlene to Tony. Obviously, if she wanted to question Charlene, she'd have to do it when Tony wasn't around. "Well, thanks, you two. That's all for now," she said.

"Detectives," Nancy heard Tony muttering as they left. "What does she think? That we're criminals or something? Why would we be slaving away here if we were thieves?"

"I agree," an unfamiliar voice just outside the door said. "Well, I guess I'm next."

"Good luck, Max," Charlene said.

Max Hudson had to be the best-looking stockboy in the world, Nancy decided when he stepped into the room. He had strong, handsome features, tousled wheat-blond hair, and a body-builder's physique. He shot Nancy a wry grin and flopped down in the chair beside the desk.

"Here I am," he announced. "What do you want to know? I'm Max, by the way."

"Max Hudson, right?" Nancy asked, double-checking the name against Kate Hayes's list.

"Yup." Max sounded totally bored.

"Well, Max," said Nancy, "I'd like to ask you a few questions about the robberies here, if you don't mind."

Max shrugged. "Go ahead," he said, leaning back in his chair.

"Max, who do you think is behind the thefts?" Nancy asked, putting the question as bluntly as she could.

"Beats me" was all Max had to say in return.

Nancy waited for him to volunteer more. He didn't

"Did you ever notice that anything was taken?" she probed.

"Nope. I only see the boxes. I don't open them. Stuff comes into the store, I put it in the stockroom. After that, I don't know a thing."

That's strange, Nancy thought. Stockboys usually unpack the boxes and log in the merchandise.

"I heard there were several boxes of jewelry taken a couple weeks ago. Did you ever see them?" she asked.

"I remember a few boxes were taken, but that's all."

"You never actually saw the jewelry, then?"

"No, just the boxes." Max couldn't be less cooperative. As he talked to Nancy, his piercing blue eyes wandered around the room like those of a schoolboy waiting for recess.

"Thanks, Max. That's all for now."

Max got up with a cursory nod and shuffled out of the room, a hint of a smile on his otherwise sullen face.

Nancy gave a quick shudder. He knew more than he was telling. Those terse replies of his told her he was holding back.

"Knock, knock." Nancy looked up and saw Trisha standing in the doorway.

"Is that everybody?" Nancy asked her.

"That's it for full-time employees," Trisha confirmed. "We used to have more, but most of them didn't work out for one reason or another. It's hard to find good help, as I'm sure you've heard."

"Well, I'd like to go over the employee records, past and present, if that's okay. And the inventory sheets."

"That's fine," Trisha said, "but not now. A big shipment just came in, and I'm going to be needing the office for the next couple of hours.

And I couldn't let you take the books out of the store without Ms. Hayes's permission."

"I guess I could come back later," Nancy suggested. "What time do you close?"

"Tonight, at eight," Trisha answered brusquely. "If you come back then, I can give you the books and teach you the security code so you can lock up when you're done."

"Great. Will you have time for a few questions then?" Nancy asked.

Trisha smiled coldly. "Sure," she said. "I'm probably your number-one suspect, right? Store manager, knows the whole operation . . ."

"Right now everyone is my number-one suspect, Trisha," Nancy said wryly.

"That's all you're going to say? Well, I'll be happy to answer any questions," Trisha told her wearily, an edge to her voice. "I want this thing solved just as much as Ms. Hayes does. My reputation's on the line, too, you know. See you later."

Nancy slid into the front seat of her Mustang and fitted the key in the ignition. The car purred into action, and Nancy rolled out of the parking lot and onto the street. What a perfect late-summer day, she thought. Too bad she'd had to spend so much time in the store.

Heading for home, Nancy considered the situation at Vanities. Tony Selby was definitely suspicious. He acted proud of his classic tough-guy

29

stance. Nancy couldn't help wondering why Charlene, who seemed so shy and sweet, would be mixed up with a guy like him. Could his looks and manner be deceiving? Of course, it was possible that he and Charlene were working together.

Max Hudson might have both the brains and know-how to organize the robberies. It was hard to tell, he'd been so tight-lipped. She remembered feeling that he was hiding something. Heading for the wealthier side of town, Nancy felt a pang of regret that she couldn't go undercover on this case.

Then there was Trisha Rapp. There was a girl with brains and know-how to spare. And she had made it clear she didn't want Nancy snooping around. But, assuming she was guilty, why would she have told Kate Hayes about the thefts in the first place? And why would she still be working in the store? Wouldn't that be risky?

As for Kate Hayes, surely a woman who owned three clothing stores might be able to run a scheme to defraud her insurance company. If she were an unethical person, that is. But judging from Vanities, Nancy decided Kate wasn't in any financial difficulty. An insurance scam seemed a slim possibility.

Nancy sighed and turned the car onto her street. So much for what she *didn't* know.

There was only one thing she was sure of. Whoever was behind the Vanities thefts couldn't be operating alone. Goods had to be trucked from place to place and turned into cash down the line. Nancy had to be looking for a partnership, not a single criminal.

Lost in thought, Nancy got out of her car and began heading up the front steps of her house. It was extremely quiet. Her dad was away on a business trip, and Hannah Gruen, the Drew family's housekeeper, was visiting her sister. Nancy knew she'd be alone that night.

"Nancy! Nancy!" A familiar voice rang out as Nancy was fishing out her keys. Turning, she watched Nikki Masters run up the walk, waving a manila envelope in her hand. There was a worried look in Nikki's soft blue eyes when she reached Nancy.

"Hi, Nikki," Nancy said, concerned. "What's wrong?"

"Oh, Nancy. Everything's wrong," Nikki blurted out. "Look at this!" She handed Nancy the large manila envelope.

Nancy reached in and pulled out a Native American–style turquoise-and-silver pendant necklace. On the back of the center stone was a large etched *Z*, almost like a lightning bolt. It was very similar to the mark she'd seen on the necklace in Vanities.

"Nice," Nancy murmured, turning the necklace and flashing it in the bright sunlight. "Why is it a problem?"

"Oh, Nancy," Nikki moaned. "My boyfriend

gave it to me," she said quickly, still trying to catch her breath. "My ex-boyfriend, I should say. I'm going to give it back to him, though."

"You mean Dan Taylor?" His name came back to Nancy from the fight she'd overheard the night before.

Nikki looked at her curiously. "Yes. How did you know?"

"I heard you arguing with him," Nancy confessed. "Want to talk about it?"

Nikki nodded her head and the two girls sat on the top step. "Oh, Nancy, love is so complicated. I mean, sometimes I get so angry with Dan I just want to kill him! And other times, all he has to do is look at me, and I melt."

"Sounds pretty intense, Nikki," Nancy said sympathetically.

"It is! I mean, Dan is a nice guy and all, but he's got a lot of problems," Nikki explained. "At first I thought I could help him, but then— I don't know. I kind of felt like I was in over my head, you know? So I told him I thought we both needed a little time apart. That's when he gave me this!" Nikki clutched the necklace in her slender fingers.

"Well, if you don't want to accept an expensive gift, you can always give it back to him," Nancy advised.

"It's more than that," Nikki explained. She looked at Nancy strangely. "I'm worried about

Dan, Nancy. He doesn't even have a job anymore."

"Does Dan have a lot of money saved up?" Nancy asked, her eyes fixed on the expensive necklace.

"No!" Nikki proclaimed. "That's what's bothering me. Oh, Nancy, I hate to say this—but I think he stole it!"

Chapter

Four

THE MINUTE Nikki said the necklace might be stolen, Nancy wondered if necklaces had been taken from Vanities.

"Can I borrow this for a while?" she asked, fingering the smooth polished silver. "Maybe I can find out where Dan got it," she explained.

"Sure," said Nikki. A tear spilled down her cheek. "Thanks."

"Come on, Nikki," Nancy said, putting her arm around her distraught friend's slender shoulders. "Just because you don't see where Dan got the money doesn't mean the necklace was stolen. Maybe his parents gave him money to buy you a gift."

Nikki ran a nervous hand through her blond hair and shook her head. "No way, Nancy. Dan's parents don't have much money. Not only that, they can't stand me."

"Maybe you'd better start from the beginning," Nancy told her, reaching out and touching her hand reassuringly.

"Okay," Nikki said, gulping back tears. "Let's see, I met Dan at Frank's one night last spring. He'd just moved to River Heights, and I thought he was wonderful. He was so good-looking, and he seemed so nice. I was thrilled when he asked me out."

Nancy nodded. Dan was really cute. Based on his looks alone, Nancy could understand why a girl would be attracted to him.

"Anyway, we started going out, and it was fantastic. Dan is really special, Nancy. Honestly. He has big dreams, but he's also sensitive and down-to-earth. He's older than me—nineteen. But I figured that was okay. Until . . ."

Nikki's voice trailed off, and her blue eyes misted over. Nancy waited patiently for her to continue.

"One day I was at a party at Jeremy Pratt's house—or should I say, mansion. Jeremy made a crack about Dan being a compulsive liar."

"That's a pretty heavy charge," Nancy said. "What did he mean?"

"That's what I wanted to know! He told me about how Dan had lied to get a job. Dan told the owner of some fancy store he knew the Pratts from the country club, and he was Jeremy's best friend. Jeremy was furious about that."

"Could it have been a misunderstanding of some kind?" Nancy asked.

"That's what I thought," Nikki said, shaking her head sadly. "But when I asked Dan about it, he froze up, and I could tell Jeremy's story was all true! Then I started thinking about other things he'd told me, about the places he said he'd traveled to, and the money he had. Oh, Nancy, it was all a pack of lies!"

"That's terrible, Nikki," Nancy murmured. "But if he felt he had to lie, he must have been awfully insecure about something."

"I know! I told Dan he didn't have to pretend with me, that I liked him for himself. But it was like he couldn't stop. Then I found out he'd lost his job—for *lying!* And I thought that was it. Jeremy was right. This guy is really messed up."

"What do your friends think about him?" Nancy asked.

Nikki rolled her blue eyes. "Robin and Lacey told me I was crazy to go out with him. They said I should drop him."

"Sounds like good advice, Nikki," Nancy suggested gently.

"But it isn't that easy, Nancy. I *love* Dan. I really love him. Lacey and Robin don't know him like I do. Yes, he's got problems, but he's not really bad or crazy or anything."

Nikki couldn't stop the tears that started spilling down her cheeks. Nancy bit her lip and decided not to offer any more opinions until she'd heard everything. Instead, she gave Nikki a tissue from her purse.

"I did try to break up with him, Nancy," Nikki managed to say through her tears. "But I guess I wasn't forceful enough. Dan told me we were meant for each other, and I should give him another chance."

"And did you?"

"Yes, but nothing changed. Even though he kept telling me his whole life was going to change soon. It didn't. He's so secretive I can't help feeling that everything he's telling me is a cover-up for something else."

"I can't tell you what to do about Dan, Nikki," Nancy said softly. "If I were you, I wouldn't assume he stole anything. But it's never a good idea, when you're trying to break up with a guy, to take gifts from him. Other than that, what can I say? Relationships are hard, sometimes they don't work out. But you'll survive. There'll be other guys. I hope that doesn't sound too uncaring. I'm just looking out for your feelings."

"I know you are, Nancy," Nikki said, letting her shoulders drop. "And I know I should break up with him. It's just that I feel like I'm letting him down when he needs me the most."

"Nikki, it sounds like he needs help, but maybe

you're not the one to give it. Have you tried talking to his parents?"

"I tried, Nancy," Nikki moaned. "They deny everything. To them, Dan has no problems whatsoever, other than me!"

Nancy was quiet, trying to think of what else she could say to comfort her friend.

"Oh! I forgot about the letter." Nikki pulled a piece of paper out of the manila envelope she was still holding. "Here. Read this."

Nancy read the note.

Nikki, this necklace reminded me of you. Soon our troubles will be over, and you'll have lots more gifts. But remember, my life is my gift to you. Please don't break up with me, Nikki. Without you, my life is over.

Yours forever,
Dan.

A cold shiver made its way up Nancy's spine. "Nikki," she said softly, "if I were you, I'd break it off with Dan. The sooner the better."

"Right on time." Checking her watch, Trisha Rapp pressed the code to open the door for Nancy.

"Everything okay?" Nancy asked as she stepped in and looked around the empty store.

"No more thefts, if that's what you mean,"

38

Trisha answered, giving Nancy a hard look.

Nancy held up the necklace she'd gotten from Nikki and showed it to Trisha. "Have you ever seen this before?" she asked.

A shadow crossed Trisha's face and disappeared just as quickly. "No," she said with a casual smile. "Ms. Hayes doesn't go for that look. She likes more modern styles. Now, if you want to take a look at those books . . ." she said as she led Nancy back to her office.

Disappointed, Nancy slipped the necklace into her pocket and followed Trisha into the office. She made herself comfortable in the office chair next to the desk.

"How long have you worked here, Trisha?" Nancy asked casually.

"Let's see. It must be six months. I got the job the first week I arrived in River Heights."

"Uh-huh. You like it here?"

Trisha made a face. "Well, it's kind of 'smallsville,' if you know what I mean. It's a little too quiet for me. No offense—I know it's your hometown—but I'm used to a little more action. I'm more of a big-town person."

Nancy didn't appreciate Trisha's attitude, but she didn't say anything. "What's your opinion of Kate Hayes?" she asked instead.

Trisha hesitated. "You want my honest opinion?" she asked. Without waiting for Nancy to answer, she said, "She's nice enough, I guess. But she's a lousy judge of character."

Nancy cocked her head to the side. "What do you mean by that?" she asked.

"See for yourself" was Trisha's only answer. "Here are the employee records. And here's the code so you can lock up when you're through. Destroy the paper after you've memorized it, okay?"

"Yup." Nancy waved as Trisha strolled out the door. Committing the five-digit code to memory, she stuffed the paper in her jeans pocket.

Through the open office door, Nancy heard Trisha leaving. Then an unearthly quiet descended on the room. She looked up at the camera overhead. It was quietly filming everything that happened in the office. She reached for the inventory list and got to work.

According to the list, there was no way to tell when any items had been stolen. The list simply recorded their purchase and noted the date they were received at the store. A later note, penciled in by Trisha, indicated what was missing.

Nancy pushed the inventory list aside and reached for the employee records. The first thing she noticed was that Trisha Rapp, with six months' service, was the longest-term employee at the store. Her out-of-state references from Colorado were all excellent.

Max Hudson and Tony Selby, on the other hand, had less than sterling recommendations. Max's former employer noted he had a tendency to show up at work late. And Tony's record indicated he could be hard to get along with and had an aggressive personality.

Apparently, Kate Hayes had hired them in spite of their lackluster pasts. So Trisha was right. Either Ms. Hayes had flaws in her judgment or something else was going on.

It was no surprise to Nancy that Charlene Rice had never held a job before. Her inexperience explained her lack of confidence.

Checking her watch, Nancy let out a sigh. It was almost time to meet Bess and George. The three of them were going to the movies. Ned was busy with his family that night, so the girls had corralled her into going with them.

Nancy finished up by turning to the last page of employee records. There she found a complete list of the people who'd worked for the store in the past. She ran her eyes down the list and got ready to close the book.

Then she stopped short.

Her breath caught in her throat. She had to stare at the name for a full ten seconds before she could really believe it. But there it was: Employed April 13 through June 30.

Dan Taylor!

Chapter

Five

N<small>ANCY SAT STARING</small> at Dan's name as thoughts and images raced through her head. The silver-and-turquoise necklace with the designer's initial Z on the back. Dan lying to get a job. Trisha Rapp saying how hard it was to find good help and that Kate Hayes had lousy judgment in people.

Dan Taylor. All the pieces fit, Nancy realized. His bizarre behavior, his desperation, his lying, and showing up with an expensive gift when he didn't have a job. Dan had to be mixed up in the thefts!

Then Nancy looked at the dates again. Dan was employed from April 13 until June 30.

According to the police reports, the thefts hadn't started until July.

Of course, Nancy thought, he could have learned the electronic security codes while he was employed at Vanities.

Assuming that was true, though, how could he have continued stealing from the store? Trisha told Nancy they'd changed the code after the very first theft. Nancy made a note to double-check.

Leaning back in Trisha's chair, Nancy couldn't help feeling unsettled. She hated to think Nikki was involved with someone who might be a thief!

Nancy took a last glance at the inventory sheets. The missing items included jewelry and belts, but none of the descriptions seemed to match the necklace Nancy had taken from Nikki.

Putting the books back in order, she grabbed her handbag and went to the front of the store. Bess and George would be waiting for her.

Well, Nancy thought as she locked up, at least she had a lead now.

The Dan Taylor coincidence couldn't just be a dead end. Could it?

"Well, there you are! We'd about given up on you," Bess scolded, her pretty face a comic mask of annoyance. "Come on, the movie starts in ten minutes."

Nancy glanced down at Bess's and George's empty checkered plates. They were at

Chomper's, the mall's best burger restaurant. "But I haven't even eaten yet," she protested.

"Well, we waited and waited, but then we figured you forgot and ate dinner on your own," George said, shrugging and counting out change for the tip.

"Sorry, guys," Nancy offered. "I got caught up in some paperwork. The case is jumping."

"Tell us on the way to the Sixplex," Bess said, hurrying her.

"Hold on, let me get something to take out. Waiter!" A young waiter approached Nancy. She quickly ordered a roast beef sandwich to go.

Bess tapped her foot impatiently. "Honestly, Nan. If I miss one second of Rob Tower's face on that screen, we're staying to see it again. You know I'm totally in love with him."

"Getting carried away, are we, Bess?" George teased, poking her cousin playfully.

"All set," said Nancy a couple of minutes later as she grabbed her sandwich from the waiter and handed him the correct change. "Let's go."

As the three half walked, half ran down the promenade, Bess told them everything she'd heard about the movie they were going to see.

"He's so dreamy! And the pool scenes are supposed to be incredible. Nan? Nancy Drew, are you listening to me at all?" Bess asked petulantly.

Nancy's gaze was fixed straight ahead. There,

across the lobby of the Sixplex, waiting at the entrance to one of the other movies, stood Charlene Rice. "Huh? Oh, yes, I'm listening. Something about a pool scene?"

"You're the worst, Nancy!" Bess giggled. "But I bet you pay attention when the movie's on!"

As they stood in line, Nancy tried to keep an eye on Charlene, but the crowds soon obscured her view.

"Three, please," said George. Nancy handed her friend the money for her ticket and glanced toward the back of the line. There was Max Hudson. He was biting his lip and looking about him anxiously.

"Listen, you guys," she told Bess and George quietly. "Charlene, the salesgirl from Vanities, and a guy are here. I want to keep an eye on them. I'll meet you inside, okay?"

"Nothing doing!" Bess whispered loudly. "Nancy, you promised me you'd check out Rob Tower."

"I know, but this case is important." Nancy searched around for some sight of Charlene. She couldn't spot her.

"Nan," George broke in. "It's Friday night. The crooks aren't likely to risk another theft so soon, are they?"

"Probably not," Nancy admitted. "Still, I feel silly going to the movies in the middle of a case."

"You won't feel silly when you see Rob Tower.

I promise," Bess said, grabbing her arm and pulling her inside.

When they emerged from the movie, Bess was too enrapt to even speak. Nancy glanced around, hoping to see Charlene and Max. Neither was near.

"It was probably just a coincidence they were here," George said.

"I guess you're right," Nancy said. "But there've been an awful lot of coincidences lately. Speaking of which—" Nancy could hardly believe her eyes.

Trisha Rapp was coming out of theater number four with a tall, burly man in a cowboy hat. The two were talking.

The man might have been about thirty, but he looked older because of the scowl on his face. Probably he didn't like the movie, Nancy guessed, wondering whether he was Trisha's boyfriend. If he was—judging by the cowboy hat— he was probably from out of town.

Trisha's green eyes flickered in Nancy's direction, but the second they made contact, Trisha turned away. Grabbing her escort's arm, she steered him off in the opposite direction. It might have been innocent enough, but Nancy couldn't shake the feeling that Trisha was avoiding her.

"Wasn't that Trisha, the manager of Vanities?" George asked, curious.

"Uh-huh. Another of my suspects. I think she was trying to avoid us."

They strolled down the promenade toward the parking lot as Nancy filled them in on all the details of the case. She also told them about Dan and Nikki's romance.

Then Bess and George piled into Bess's car and drove off, while Nancy jumped into her Mustang and headed home. The movie had been fun, but her mind was still very much on Dan Taylor and the problems at Vanities.

Nancy got out of the car and breathed in deeply. The flowers growing beside the Drew house filled the air with a heady mixture of fragrances. Poor Nikki, Nancy thought. She wasn't going to be happy to learn what Nancy had found out about Dan.

Of course, Nancy didn't have any hard evidence against Dan. It was entirely possible Dan had bought the jewelry with money that was rightfully his. Possible, but not likely.

The Masterses' house was dark. Nancy figured the family was out for the evening. She'd have to talk to Nikki the next day.

Nancy was digging out her key when she saw something out of the corner of her eye. She turned only her head, just in time to see a figure emerge from the bushes in front of the Masterses' house next door.

In the dark she couldn't tell who it was, but

Nancy herself stood out in the brilliant yellow of the overhead porch light. Seeing her, the figure was startled, then fled down the street, passing under a street lamp.

In the pool of light from the lamp, Nancy made out a distinctive eagle patch on the arm of a jacket. The person fleeing from Nikki's darkened house was Dan Taylor!

Chapter

Six

THE MINUTE Dan was out of sight, Nancy dashed for her car. She hopped in the Mustang and sped off, keeping her eyes open for Dan.

But by the time Nancy reached the end of the block, Dan had vanished. Circling the area, Nancy hoped to catch a glimpse of Dan's old blue bomber. He had to have parked it somewhere nearby.

As Nancy searched the blocks around hers, she wondered why Dan didn't want to be seen. Was he afraid of making Nikki more angry by hanging around, or was it something more?

Finally she spotted him at the next corner, just

opening his car door. Nancy waited at the end of the block until he pulled out.

Nancy carefully followed Dan as he drove to Ridgeview Road, past the town center, and into an older, run-down section of town. He pulled up in front of a video arcade across from the old Ridgeview Motel. Nancy sank down in the driver's seat, peering out the window to see Dan glance around quickly before going inside the arcade.

Judging from the rough-looking guys who were going in and out of the arcade, Nancy decided not to enter. No sense sticking out like a sore thumb.

She pulled into the motel parking lot and turned off her headlights. From the lot she had a bird's-eye view of the arcade's entrance.

It didn't take more than a minute for Dan to reemerge. And who should come out with him but Max Hudson! Nancy felt her whole body tighten and become instantly alert. What if Max and Dan were working the thefts together?

Just as that thought came to Nancy, her eyes widened in horror. Max had thrown Dan against the wall and was hitting him! Dan put his arms up in front of his face and curled up to protect his stomach. As far as Nancy could tell, he wasn't trying to fight back.

In any case he would have been no match for the muscular Max, who obviously spent a lot of time at the gym working out.

Nancy reached for the car handle to open the door. But before she could get out of her car, Max had stopped. Evidently he'd decided Dan had had enough.

Nursing his right fist in his left hand, Max headed back inside the arcade, leaving Dan slumped against the wall, his head buried in both hands. People milled around him, but they seemed afraid to interfere.

Nancy got out of the car and hurried over to Dan. His face was already swelling. When Nancy met his eyes she saw a look on Dan's face that was terrified and confused. Her heart went out to him, and in that instant she understood why Nikki Masters was attracted to Dan Taylor. There was something so innocent and so needy in those eyes.

"Wh-who are you?" he stammered.

"I'm a friend," Nancy answered. "Are you all right?"

"I—I think so," he said, feeling his face for painful spots. When his fingers reached his nose, he said, "Don't think it's broken, anyway."

"You're going to have a black eye, that's for sure." Nancy held out a helping hand as he struggled to his feet. "Here, take these," she added, giving him a few clean tissues from her jacket pocket.

Without a word, he took them and held them to his nose.

"What happened? Why was that guy hitting you?" Nancy ventured.

The words seemed to shake Dan out of his confusion and back into his hard shell. He pulled himself upright and eyed her warily. "You're Nikki's neighbor. You followed me here, didn't you?" he said slowly.

Nancy thought it would be better for her to be straightforward. "Yes, I did," she said. "I saw you sneaking around Nikki's house, and I thought you might be a burglar."

"A burglar?" he said, shaking his head in disbelief. "I'm Nikki's boyfriend!" Dan paused. Then he gave Nancy an intensely cold stare and went on. "I have a great idea. You mind your own business, and I'll mind mine, okay?"

"I was just being a good neighbor," Nancy said, trying to sound affronted. She wondered what exactly was making Dan Taylor so wary.

"Never mind," Dan said, backing off. "Sorry I was rude. I'm just—you know," he said, touching his face. "Thanks for the help," he added.

"You should get some ice on your eye," Nancy suggested gently. "It would help the swelling."

"Yeah, good idea," he said with a weary nod. "Thanks."

Nancy realized there was no sense in her hanging around any longer. Nothing was going to happen while Dan knew she was there.

"Take care of yourself," she said, and made her way back to her car.

Dan nodded and stood there, his eyes fixed on her. Was he actually going to go back in the arcade, with Max Hudson still inside?

Crossing the street, she got into her car and drove off. In her rearview mirror, she could see Dan in the neon light from the arcade, staring at her, making sure she was really leaving before making a move.

"Well, I don't trust you either, Dan Taylor," she said out loud, turning back and heading for home. "And don't think you've seen the last of me. Not by a long shot."

When Nancy turned onto her street, the first thing that caught her eye was that there were lights on in the Masterses' house. After parking her car, Nancy went over and rapped quietly on the door.

Nikki opened it quickly when she saw it was Nancy. She put her finger to her lips. "Hi, Nancy," she whispered. "My folks are asleep. Let's talk out here."

"Where were you, Nikki? I wanted to talk to you."

"Mom and Dad went out tonight," Nikki explained with a worried look. "I was alone in the house, and I was afraid to answer the door. I thought it might be Dan."

Nikki Masters was smart for her age. If she had

let Dan in, he would have been at her all night, begging her to get back together, weakening her resolve. "Not a bad move," Nancy admitted.

"He was here—he rang the bell over and over. He must have tried for half an hour."

"I saw him," Nancy told her with a sad expression. "Nikki, there's something I've got to tell you about Dan."

Nikki must have seen from the look in Nancy's eyes that what she had to tell her was serious. "Oh, no, it's something bad, isn't it, Nancy?" Nikki backed up a few steps and braced herself.

There was no easy way to tell the girl the truth. Nancy decided to plunge in. "I saw Dan getting beat up tonight, Nikki. By a guy named Max Hudson. Ever hear of him?"

"Yes," Nikki said with a shudder. "He's kind of a friend of Dan's. Well, more like an acquaintance, I'd guess you could say." Then the news about Dan's being beaten up began to sink in. A tear fell from Nikki's eye and ran down her cheek.

Nancy put an arm around her shoulder. "Do you have any idea why Max would want to beat up Dan, Nikki?" Nancy asked.

Nikki wiped the tears from her eyes. "Oh, Nancy, Dan doesn't seem to be able to stay out of trouble, does he? Is he okay?"

"Well, he's got a black eye and a couple of cuts, but he'll be okay." Nancy decided not to tell

Nikki about the thefts at Vanities and Dan's possible connection. For one thing, she had no proof that he was involved. For another, she didn't want to upset her friend any more than she already was.

"Nikki," Nancy said gently, "I hope you'll stay far away from Dan from now on."

"I will," Nikki promised. "Nancy, do you think Dan will get his life back together?"

"I hope so," Nancy said. "Good night, Nikki. Sleep well."

Nancy awoke late after a night of troubled dreams. She went down to the kitchen and poured herself a cold glass of orange juice and rubbed the cobwebs from her eyes. Outside, the day had begun brilliantly.

The memory of Nikki and Dan walking hand in hand in the park the other night came back to her. What was happening to them now was so sad.

Nancy understood what Nikki saw in Dan, but she also knew that Nikki had good sense. She wouldn't have fallen for a guy if he'd shown signs of having big problems in the beginning. Dan Taylor must have changed a whole lot in the last three months, maybe into an entirely new person. The question was, why?

Nancy was pondering the question when the phone rang. "Hello?" she said, lifting the receiver.

"Nancy?" came the agitated voice on the other end of the line. "This is Trisha Rapp."

"Trisha, hi," said Nancy, glancing at her clock. It was close to ten.

"I think you'd better get over here right away." Trisha's voice was shaky.

"Where are you?" Nancy asked.

"At the store—where else would I be?" Trisha answered.

"Trisha, what's the matter?" Nancy asked calmly.

"I'll tell you what's wrong, Nancy." Trisha's voice had a hard edge. "There was another theft here during the night. A *big* one."

Chapter

Seven

DUMB, DUMB, DUMB!" Nancy banged her hand on the steering wheel as she drove to the mall. How could she have let this happen? Why hadn't she staked out the place?

Nancy let out a breath of frustration. She had blown it royally, and was she ever going to hear about it from Kate Hayes when she got to Vanities!

Nancy pushed through the glass entrance to the store. Kate Hayes was behind the opened cash register, poring over a list that Trisha Rapp held out to her.

"Nancy. Good morning. Or should I say, I

wish it were good." Kate's greeting was far from cheery. Trisha just nodded.

"We lost a lot this time. A lot," Kate said, with a sad shake of her head. "A shipment of Bob Broward separates. Every piece of jade in the store."

"And more," Trisha added regretfully, handing her boss yet another list. "I can't find these things, either."

"Was there any sign of a forced entry?" Nancy asked.

Kate shook her head. "No, there wasn't," she answered tersely.

Nancy began walking around the store and checking out the employees. Tony Selby was in a black mood, his mouth set, his eyes on Charlene. For her part, Charlene seemed unusually jumpy. She kept dropping things, bumping into people, and apologizing profusely.

Max Hudson seemed to be working hard, even with his bandaged right hand. He had been out late the night before. Had he finished the night up at Vanities?

Nancy edged back to the stockroom, making her way toward the office. As she did, she heard Kate Hayes on the phone inside. From the sound of her conversation, she was talking to her insurance company, and she obviously didn't like what she was hearing.

"But I tell you, the jackets really did disappear!" the store owner was complaining as Nancy peeked in through the door. "Do you think I made it all up?"

Kate held her hand to her forehead while she waited for their reply. "Please," she said, after a moment. "I know we're having special problems here, and believe me, we're trying to get to the bottom of them. But if you drop my policy now, I'll be finished!"

If Kate Hayes was inventing these thefts, she was doing a great acting job. And if she'd done it to scam her insurance company, the trick didn't seem to be working. From what Nancy was hearing, they weren't buying a word of her story.

Nancy heard her hang up with a slam of the receiver. She knocked softly on the half-open door and walked in.

Kate was rubbing her temples, and her eyes were squeezed shut. "Come in, Nancy," she murmured, without looking up.

"Are you all right?" Nancy asked.

"I'm afraid not," Ms. Hayes answered with a wince. "It seems I've reached the limits on my coverage. My insurance company is acting as if I'm trying to pull something funny. Essentially, if there are any more thefts, Vanities is out of business, and so am I."

Kate Hayes lifted her head and tried to compose herself. It didn't work. For all her pride, she looked defeated.

"We'll figure this out, Kate," Nancy said, mustering an assurance she didn't really feel. "I promise you we will."

"Well, I certainly hope so. Meanwhile, I'm going to pay my insurance agent a personal call. I think we need to talk face-to-face." She stood up and reached for her elegant silk jacket. "Good luck to all of us," she murmured hopelessly.

After Kate left, Nancy walked to her desk and glanced at the open phone directory. There was the number of the insurance company. More proof that Kate Hayes had not been acting.

"You know," Trisha said, standing in the doorway with an angry scowl on her face, "you have a lot of nerve!"

Nancy's eyes widened. "Oh?" she answered calmly.

"Yes. You act like you can solve these problems, but I don't think you can," she scolded. "You'll be happy to hear I didn't tell Ms. Hayes that you were at the movies instead of on the job. I probably should have!"

So Trisha had seen her! "Thanks, Trisha," Nancy said quietly. "I really appreciate that." An apologetic smile passed over Nancy's face. No matter how irritating Trisha was being right now, antagonizing her wasn't going to get Nancy anywhere.

As Trisha was about to walk away, Nancy stepped around the desk. "Trisha, wait," she called out. "What can you tell me about a guy named Dan Taylor?"

Trisha started. She blinked her green eyes a few times before answering. "Dan Taylor?" she asked finally. "What about him? He used to work here, but that was before all this stuff started happening."

"I know that," Nancy said, stepping out of Kate's office and standing next to Trisha in the hallway. "But what do you know about him?"

"Well, I know one thing for sure. He's not the guy you're after. Frankly, he's not smart enough or nervy enough to be a thief. That's my opinion, anyway."

"You didn't like him, I take it."

Trisha scowled. "Actually, I fired him. He was totally unreliable." She shook her head. "He was even late for his first interview here. The only reason he got hired is that he knew the Pratt family. When Kate heard that, she insisted on hiring him. He was a nice guy, but totally in the ozone, if you know what I mean. Sort of flaky."

"Why did you fire him?" Nancy asked.

"I caught him lying—right to my face. He was always lying. He always had a story about why he was late or why he couldn't work on weekends. I knew it, but I couldn't do anything about it. Then one day he called in sick, and I saw him taking a girl out to lunch. That was the end. When he finally came in, I fired him on the spot. I told Ms.

Hayes about it later. If I'd asked her permission, she would have said to give him another chance. I told you that she's a bad judge of character."

Nancy nodded. Trisha's decision seemed a bit harsh, but apparently Dan had pushed his luck too far.

"I've got to get back to work now," Trisha said. "And if you want my advice, you should, too." With that, Trisha took off down the hall.

"Watch out!" The man's voice was loud and sounded irritated. Nancy ducked back into Kate's office doorway and peered down the hall. Max Hudson was barreling down the corridor, carrying a stack of cartons on his shoulder. He appeared to have come from the loading docks under the mall.

Tony Selby, holding a sheaf of papers, was about to run into him. He jumped out of Max's way, and headed for the bulletin board at the rear of the hall. Once there, he started busily tacking up papers.

"Do you mind if I ask you where you were last night?" Nancy asked him.

Tony looked at her strangely. "Um, I was home. Sick."

"Was anyone with you?" Nancy prodded him.

"Nope," he answered with a shrug.

"You were sick, huh? You seem fine now."

Tony shot her a bored smile. "I got better," he said.

"Well, nice talking to you."

Nancy headed for the stockroom. She wanted to talk to Max, and she hoped he'd be more cooperative.

Max Hudson was slicing cartons open with a packing knife. So he was lying when he said he never opened the cartons, Nancy thought to herself. "I saw you at the arcade last night, Max," Nancy said casually. "How long were you there?"

Max frowned. "All night," he answered, and set to work again.

"Really?" she asked incredulously. "You sure you weren't at the Sixplex?"

That caught him off guard. But Max recovered in an instant. "Oh, yeah," he said casually. "I was just passing by, and I went in to say hello to a friend who works there."

"They let you in without a ticket?"

"Yeah," he answered.

"I see," said Nancy lightly. Obviously, Max was not telling her everything, and he must have a good reason for lying.

Passing from the stockroom back into the store, Nancy watched Charlene nervously checking racks of dresses.

"Hi, Charlene," Nancy began.

Charlene acted as if she'd just gotten an electric shock. "Oh, hi, Nancy," she said, spinning around.

"I'm asking everyone the same question," Nancy began.

"You mean, where was I last night?" Charlene finished for her.

Nancy nodded. "I was at the movies until about eleven," Charlene explained. "Then I went home. You can call my parents if you don't believe me."

"I believe you, Charlene," Nancy told her. "Which movie did you see?"

"High Speed," she told Nancy.

"Sounds interesting. What's it about?"

"About? Oh, it's a police story. There's a jewel heist from a museum, and the cops chase the thieves all over the world. . . ." Charlene's voice trailed off.

Nancy had seen *High Speed*. It was a love story. Not a policeman in it. And Charlene had been standing outside *The Return of the Spider People*. Obviously, she hadn't seen either movie.

"I'd like to talk, but I really should be behind the counter," Charlene finally said.

"Sure. Go ahead," Nancy said. There was no sense confronting Charlene head on. Besides, all the employees at Vanities were being so evasive that they all seemed guilty.

After she checked the back door and the storeroom and didn't find any clues, Nancy left Vanities and headed home. She planned to take a quick nap so that later she could spend the night staking the place out.

Once she was home Nancy checked the answering machine in her bedroom. There were two messages. The first was from Ned.

"Hi, Nan. Well, it's Saturday and I know we talked about tonight, but I haven't heard from you. I guess you're busy with that new case of yours. I sure would like to see you, though. Summer's almost gone, and so am I. Call me, okay?"

Nancy only hoped Ned wouldn't be disappointed with their date that night. A mall stakeout was probably not the kind of date he had in mind.

The second message was from Nikki, and she sounded positively frantic:

"Nancy—it's me— I'm scared, Nancy, and I— Something just happened, and—please, come over as soon as you get this message! Please!"

In no time Nancy was out the door. Whatever had happened to Nikki, it sounded serious. She only hoped she wasn't too late!

Chapter

Eight

Nancy flew across the lawn to the Masterses'
house and leaned on the doorbell. In a few
minutes a shaken Nikki came to the door. A wave
of relief coursed through Nancy. At least she was
in one piece. On the phone she'd sounded as if
she was in real danger.

"Thank goodness you're here!" Nikki began,
drawing Nancy inside and shutting the front
door behind them. "Dan was waiting for me
when I left the house this morning. He was hiding
behind the bushes and jumped out to greet me.
Oh, Nancy, he looks terrible! His whole face was
swollen, and his eye—"

Nancy led Nikki over to the sofa and sat her

down. "Take it easy," she said soothingly. "Everything's going to be all right."

"He was all disheveled, and he had this wild look in his eye," Nikki went on. From the way she described the scene, Nancy realized Nikki was seeing it all again in her mind. "He tried to get me to take another gift from him. He kept insisting and insisting."

"What was it?"

"I don't know, I didn't take it," Nikki answered. "I know you would have wanted to see it, Nancy, but I couldn't. He would have thought I wanted him back again, and I don't! I feel for Dan and everything, but I don't know how to help him, and I'm starting to be *afraid* of him. Not that I actually think he'd hurt me, but—"

"When people are unstable, Nikki, you never know," Nancy cautioned.

"Not Dan," Nikki insisted. "He loves me. He would never hurt me."

"Did you get a look at the gift?" Nancy asked. "It could be important."

Nikki stared at her in confusion. "Actually, now that I think of it, I'm not even sure it was a gift. It was a big fat envelope," she said nervously. "He tried to give it to me about six times. He said that I wouldn't even have to open it. Weird, huh? No wonder my friends are so worried about me and my relationship with him."

Nikki burst into bitter tears. Nancy could tell

her neighbor was torn between caring for Dan and protecting herself. "Oh, Nancy," she begged. "Can you do anything? Talk to his parents or something? They won't speak to me. Please," Nikki begged again.

Along with helping her friend, an excursion to Dan's house might be very revealing, Nancy decided. "All right, Nikki, I'll go over there today. Meantime, I think you should get out a little. Isn't there some safe way to have fun? Someplace where there are lots of people around?"

"It's funny you should mention that." Nikki smiled wistfully. "Jeremy Pratt is throwing a party tonight. Robin and Lacey offered to pick me up and walk me there and back, and I said no. But I'll call them and tell them I changed my mind."

"I take it Dan isn't invited," Nancy concluded.

"No way," Nikki said with a laugh. "That's why Lacey and Robin thought I should go."

"You should—definitely!" Nancy said.

"Well, I guess I'll call them, then," Nikki said, getting to her feet. She looked worlds better than when Nancy had come in. The color was back in her cheeks, and there was a spring in her step. Suddenly Nikki looked sixteen again, fresh and radiant.

"I'll talk to you tomorrow," Nancy told her. "You can fill me in on your night out, and I'll give you the story on Mr. and Mrs. Taylor."

"Right." Nikki waved goodbye to her at the door and went back inside.

As she went down the Masterses' porch steps, Nancy swore to herself that she was going to help Nikki Masters out of the mess she was in, no matter what. But to do that, she had to find out what was really going on in Dan Taylor's life.

Nancy wondered what Dan was doing with that envelope. Guys who write love letters normally want girls to read them. What could Dan have meant when he said "You don't even have to open it, just take it"?

As Nancy was letting herself into her house, the phone was ringing. She ran to pick it up.

"Hello?"

"Ned!" Nancy said jubilantly. "I was just about to call you."

"Great," came the warm response. "So are we on for tonight?"

"We are. But there's just one thing. I'm on the job tonight."

"Oh. Does that mean you need to be alone? Or do you want some company?"

Nancy's face brightened. "Ned, you're a sweetheart. I was hoping you'd offer. I'm going to be staking out Vanities. I have a feeling nothing will happen, but I can't chance it. There was another theft last night. So I'm hoping it'll be real quiet. We'd be all alone. . . ."

"Hmmm. Sounds pretty perfect. What time should I pick you up?"

"I'll meet you at the mall. There's an ice-cream shop opposite Vanities. Nine o'clock?"

"I'll be there."

"Great." Nancy hung up the phone and picked up the River Heights phone book to look for the phone number for Dan Taylor's parents. Nancy dialed and waited. The phone rang on and on, but there was no answer. Nancy hung up and decided to try to reach them later.

Why hadn't Dan asked Nikki to open that envelope? That question was dominating Nancy's thoughts as she went to the kitchen to fix herself a late lunch. If only Nikki had taken it. Whatever was in that envelope might have given Nancy the piece she needed to complete her puzzle.

She was on her way to the dining room when the doorbell rang. Nancy set her sandwich down on the table and ran to the front door. George and Bess were standing on the porch, their faces flushed.

"Hi, Nan," they both gasped, forcing their way past her into the house. Bess plopped down on the sofa, breathing hard, while George paced the living room.

"Nancy!" George cried, the first to get her wind. "Wait till you hear what we saw!"

Bess had recovered sufficiently to take over. "We decided to do a little snooping of our own, so we went to Vanities. I tried on some truly incredible stuff, by the way."

"Never mind that!" George cut her off. "We saw something you should know about!"

"Remember that girl with the blond hair you pointed out at the movie theater?" Bess asked.

"Trisha. Yes?"

"Well, her boyfriend came into the store while we were there. The one with the cowboy hat," George went on.

"We saw them kissing when they thought no one was looking," Bess added with a grin.

"Hmmm," Nancy nodded, impressed. "Did you find out anything about him?"

Bess sat forward. "He's from Denver, it turns out."

"Denver?" Nancy said, narrowing her eyes and trying to put things together.

"Wait!" Bess practically jumped up on the sofa now. "That's not the incredible thing we saw! That guy Max, do you know the one we mean? Muscles out to here?" Bess outlined invisible biceps on her own arms. "He was at the movies last night."

"I know exactly who you mean," Nancy said.

George continued the story. "He passed a note to Charlene, the salesgirl who got yelled at that first day we were there. We saw him give it to her."

"And when she read it, she practically passed out!" Bess finished. "She looked super scared after that. Right, George?"

George nodded. "Terrified."

71

"Can you believe it?" Bess went on. "Nan, I bet those two are the thieves. They've got to be!"

"Not so fast, Bess," Nancy said. "That's not exactly conclusive evidence." She paused. "But I sure would like to get my hands on that note."

"Gee, Nan," Bess said, crestfallen. "I thought we'd solved your case for you."

"Well, you certainly have helped and probably provided a good lead—" Nancy began. But she never got to finish her thought.

At that moment, with a crash, the front window shattered.

The girls shielded their faces from the flying shards as a brick landed on the living-room floor.

Once the last shards of glass had fallen, Nancy ran to the window. Whoever had thrown the brick was nowhere to be seen.

"There's a note tied to it!" George cried.

Nancy bent down and picked up the brick. She unwrapped the note. Written in a crude, childish scrawl was a message.

Next time this brick won't just break a window! Back off, Nancy Drew!

Chapter

Nine

W HO DO YOU THINK it was, Nan?" George asked, her eyes wide with shock.

Before Nancy could answer, Bess jumped in. "It's the guy with the cowboy hat, I just know it! He has a dangerous kind of look in his eye. It's him and that girl Trisha! I feel it in my bones! Or maybe it was Max and Charlene," she finished weakly.

"Oh, Bess," George said, rolling her eyes. "You've been watching too many movies. Right, Nan? Nan?"

Nancy was staring down at the broken glass at her feet, lost in thought. "You know," she murmured softly, "the problem is that I'm zeroing in on two cases at once. Maybe Dan Taylor threw the brick. He might think I'm meddling with his relationship with Nikki. Or it could be someone trying to warn me off the Vanities case."

"How can you be so calm about something like this?" Bess asked heatedly.

"Well, Bess," Nancy replied with a hint of a smile. "I'm not exactly thrilled about someone throwing a brick through my window. But at least it shows me that I'm making progress. I'm making somebody nervous. And nervous people make mistakes."

Jumping up, Nancy went to the phone. "I'm going to call a glazier and do some cleaning up. Why don't you two go over to Vanities? Do a little snooping around before they close. See if anybody looks nervous."

The glazier had told Nancy he'd be at her house by six, but at seven-fifteen he still hadn't shown up. Nancy considered forgetting the whole thing and just leaving, but with her dad away on business and Hannah Gruen not due back from visiting her sister until the next day, she knew she had to stay and wait. She just hoped he'd be finished in time for her to meet Ned at nine at the mall.

Finally, at seven-thirty, the glazier pulled up in an old pickup.

"Sorry I'm late," he said to her through the broken window as he stood on the front porch.

The glazier raised his eyebrows and assessed the damage. "This is a big job," he said. "Odd-shaped pane. It's gonna take me a while, okay?"

What could Nancy do? "Okay," she said. She knew that if she didn't show up right at nine, Ned would start the stakeout without her, but she had hoped to stop by the Taylors' house first to try to talk to Dan's parents.

At eight the window man was still getting his tools out and sipping a cup of hot coffee he'd asked Nancy to make for him. Was she going to have to skip the visit to the Taylors? She hoped not.

Looking out the broken window, Nancy saw a cab pulling up in front of her house. A door opened and out stepped Hannah Gruen.

"Hannah!" Nancy cried happily, going out to help the housekeeper with her luggage. "You came home early!"

"What's this?" Hannah said, indicating the space where the window should have been.

"Oh, someone threw a brick through the window, that's all," Nancy said, with a wink and a hug. "Welcome home! Did you have a good time with your family?"

"You're on a new case?" Hannah asked with a knowing nod.

"You bet I am," Nancy said as she lifted Hannah's bags and walked toward the house. "And I'm especially glad to see you because I need to go out right away."

"Go!" Hannah said with a wry smile, when they reached the front door. "You can tell me all about it in the morning."

"Thanks," Nancy said. She picked up her sea green cotton sweater and her purse and flew to her car. If the Taylors' light was on, she'd take a chance and ring their bell. If not, she'd head on to the mall to meet Ned.

After looking up their address on her local map, Nancy found the Taylors' house in a development on the far side of town. As she pulled up in front of their house, Nancy was pleased that the light was on.

She parked her car and walked up to the front door. The bushes needed some trimming, but all in all the house seemed well kept. Taking a breath, she rang the bell.

"Hello?" a woman's puzzled voice called. "Who is it?"

"Mrs. Taylor?" Nancy asked through the closed door. "I'm a friend of Dan's. Can I talk to you for a minute?"

A slender woman of about forty-five opened the door. She was wearing jeans and was drying her hands on a dish towel. "Come in," she said, holding the door open.

"My name is Nancy, Mrs. Taylor."

"Hello, Nancy. That's my husband, Ernie, over there. And I'm Marie."

A man of about fifty was lying on the sofa, watching a sitcom on TV. When Nancy stepped into the living room, he nodded once quickly and went back to his program.

"He loves that show," Dan's mother said. "Let's talk in the kitchen. I can get you something to drink. A soda? Juice?"

"Juice would be fine," Nancy answered.

"So, what was it you wanted to talk about?" Marie asked once she had led Nancy through the cramped but comfortable house to the kitchen.

"Dan," Nancy answered simply. She looked straight at Mrs. Taylor.

Marie Taylor raised an eyebrow and looked Nancy over. "Oh, I understand," she cooed. "You like Dan. Is that it?"

"Well, yes," Nancy said. She felt bad about letting her get the wrong idea, but it was necessary.

"I'm very happy to hear there's someone else in Dan's life. He's been going out with this girl Nikki, but I can't stand her. She's stuck-up and too young for him. She really put Danny through the grinder, that one."

"Well, I'm just getting to know him, and I thought it might be nice to meet you."

Not only did Mrs. Taylor swallow this, she seemed overjoyed. "He's a wonderful boy, Nancy. We're very proud of him," she gushed, setting a glass of apple juice on the table and motioning for Nancy to sit. "Not many boys have achieved what Danny has."

Nancy smiled pleasantly but tilted her head

questioningly. "Dan's so modest," she murmured. "I guess I don't know much about his, um, achievements."

"Oh, well, he's a real success at that store. He's only been there a short time, and he already has a very responsible position. They send him on business trips, and he does a lot of decision making for them. Oh, my, Danny's got a real future there. He's good friends with the store manager, and everybody there loves him." Marie Taylor was beaming.

"Do you mean at Vanities?" Nancy ventured.

"Yes. It's a lovely store. I walked by once, but I felt strange about going in. Danny doesn't like it when I interfere in his life. Boys are like that. But I'm so pleased to meet you," she said, still beaming. "That other one, Nikki. What a liar. She was always calling me up to tell me all kinds of things about Danny."

Nancy wasn't sure how to play this. But she knew one thing: someone had to alert Mrs. Taylor to the fact that her son was in trouble. Dan's mother had obviously been taken in by his lies.

"You've got a lot more maturity about you than she does, Nancy, and you're every bit as pretty. I don't want to pry, but how did you and Danny meet?"

Nancy wasn't about to tell Mrs. Taylor about the night before and how she had really met Dan Taylor. "Mrs. Taylor," she said gently, "I've got to level with you. I'm worried about Danny. That's why I'm here."

Marie Taylor's features darkened. "What's the matter? Is something wrong?" Maybe underneath all that overdone pride, Mrs. Taylor sensed the truth—that Dan wasn't the big success he claimed to be.

"Have you noticed anything strange about Dan lately?" Nancy asked gently.

"Strange?" Dan's mother looked confused. "Oh! You mean the bruises? He got those yesterday, Nancy. He was out of town for the day on business. Would you believe a shelf fell on top of him at the store he was visiting? Isn't that something!" Marie laughed nervously. "You poor kid. You probably saw those bruises and thought he'd been beaten up by somebody!"

"If he was in trouble, you'd want to help him, wouldn't you?" Nancy was leaning across the table, her eyes fixed on Dan's mother.

"What are you talking about? There's no trouble, Nancy!" his mother told her. She sat up straighter in her chair. "The only problem Danny ever had was that girl Nikki. She had him so confused he didn't know what he was doing. Then she dumped him, just out of cruelty. I'm so glad he's met somebody else." Mrs. Taylor gave Nancy a sad smile.

Nancy finished her apple juice and sighed. Dan's mother already had made up her mind, and a few hard truths about Dan weren't going to change anything. There was no way she'd be able to give Nancy any honest information.

"Will Dan be home soon?" Nancy asked. Her last hope was to have a long talk with Dan. She didn't believe he was bad, deep down, but he certainly was in some kind of trouble.

"He said something about going to a party at Jeremy Pratt's house tonight," Mrs. Taylor told Nancy. "He and that Pratt boy are best friends, you know."

Nancy froze solid. Jeremy Pratt's? Nikki was going to be at Jeremy's party. She was probably there right now!

Nancy stood up and grabbed her purse. "Thanks for reminding me. I was supposed to meet Dan there. Do you have a phone book? I must have left the address in my other bag."

"Oh, certainly, dear," Mrs. Taylor said, hurrying to get a phone book from under a pile of clipped coupons on the kitchen counter.

"Patton—Peters—here! Pratt! Riverview Drive," Nancy murmured. "Well, sorry I have to run. It was very nice meeting you!"

Nancy bounded out of the kitchen and made for the front door.

As she left she heard Dan's mother talking to her husband. "Look at her run," she was saying. "That girl's in love with our Danny, no doubt about it. And she seems very nice, too."

With a wince, Nancy shut the car door and started her engine. She pulled the Mustang out onto the street and blazed away from the Taylors'. Gripping the wheel, she drove across town, as fast as she could, to an area close to her own house.

The sooner she got there, the better. Dan was in trouble and desperate to hold on to Nikki. Nikki Masters was confused and upset. If those two were in the same place at the same time, there was no telling what might happen!

Chapter

Ten

WHEN NANCY PULLED INTO the Pratts' long circular driveway, there were dozens of cars already parked there. One of them was Dan's old blue bomber. It looked out of place in the row of expensive cars that the rest of Jeremy's crowd owned.

Nancy checked her digital watch—9:33. She hoped Ned was watching the store and hadn't given up on her. Well, it wasn't the first time a case had kept them apart. Nancy knew that Ned would understand. The party was in full swing, judging by the music and the sounds of laughter.

"Hi," Nancy said to a group of kids hanging out on the steps in front of the huge double mahogany door. They were mostly younger than Nancy, and she didn't recognize any of them. "Is Jeremy around?" she asked them, figuring she should introduce herself to the host first.

"Sure. You a new girlfriend of his?" one of the guys asked, eyeing her appreciatively. Nancy barely suppressed a giggle. Despite his attempt to look older, the guy had to be all of fifteen.

"No, I've never even met him," she admitted. "I'd like to, though. Is he around?"

"He said he had to go to the store to get some more soda," a girl with long blond hair explained. "He just left five minutes ago."

"Oh." Nancy bit her lip. She didn't really want to crash the party without first meeting Jeremy. "I feel a little funny about just walking in," she said, hesitating on the steps.

"Ah, don't worry about it," the fifteen-year-old Romeo told her. "If he got a look at you, he'd invite you for sure. Go on in. And, hey, save a dance for me later, okay? Name's Jay."

"Sure thing, Jay." Nancy winked and went inside.

Jeremy Pratt sure knew how to throw a party. The house was packed solid with people. There had to be a hundred kids—at least. Nancy wondered why he'd gone out—there was lots to drink and eat. Strange. Maybe he just wanted to be prepared in case the party went on all night. From the look of things, Nancy thought, it just might.

Nancy looked around at the crowd. There wasn't a soul she knew. There was no sign of Dan or Nikki, either. She wondered if they were together.

Over in the corner sat two girls, talking in serious and hushed tones. One was a pretty and ethereal redhead, with her hair done in a single braid. She had a dusting of freckles across her nose, visible even in the half-light. Her friend was also pretty, with blunt-cut dark hair and huge dark eyes.

On a hunch she went over to them. "Excuse me," she said, crouching down beside them. "My name's Nancy Drew. I'm looking for Nikki Masters. She's a friend of mine. Have you seen her?"

The two girls looked at each other, then at Nancy. Then the dark-haired one said, "Nikki told us about you, Nancy. I'm Robin Fisher, and this is Lacey Dupree. We're Nikki's friends."

"Have you seen Nikki?" she repeated. "I spotted Dan Taylor's car outside, and I'm worried."

"You're not half as worried as we are," Robin broke in anxiously. "Right, Lacey?"

"Right," the other girl agreed. "She told us she could handle it, but we're not so sure."

"Handle what? I don't understand." Nancy looked from one of them to the other. Was something going on between Nikki and Dan right this very minute?

"He wanted to talk to her in private. They're

out back, on the patio," Robin explained. "Alone. They're having another 'last conversation.' I swear, that Dan is the most persistent person in the entire universe."

"And creepy, too," Lacey shuddered. "But Nikki has a soft spot for him. I think she just feels sorry for him. Still, I think we should get her. They've been out there a long time."

"Give them a little more time," Robin said, overruling her. "Maybe she's letting him down easy—I hope."

Nancy checked her watch. 9:55. "Okay." She nodded. "At ten, we go out and get her. I have a few things I want to talk to Dan about, too."

"If you want my opinion," Robin said, cocking her pretty head to one side, "he's got a lot of nerve just showing up here. Jeremy can't stand him, and Dan knows it. It's a good thing Jeremy was out when Dan got here or there would have been real trouble."

"Okay, let's go get her," Lacey said, getting up after a few minutes. "I think Dan's had more than enough time alone with Nikki."

Nancy followed Robin and Lacey to the beveled-glass French doors that led outside. The three of them stepped out onto a large slate terrace overhung by an awning and lighted by lanterns. A set of slate steps led down to the backyard. A grove of maple trees offered shade from the moonlight.

The girls looked around for Nikki and Dan, but the terrace seemed deserted. They split up and strolled to opposite ends of the terrace and then out into the garden.

"They've gone," Robin announced when the three met back at the terrace steps.

"I know," Nancy agreed, a worried look clouding her pretty face.

Suddenly a strident voice came from right behind them. "Looking for the loving couple?"

Nancy spun around and saw a stunning girl with dark features and a sly smile that seemed to say, "I have a secret."

"Brittany!" Lacey cried. "You nearly scared us to death!"

"You scare easily, don't you?" Brittany said.

"You were out here, spying on their whole conversation, weren't you?" Robin demanded hotly.

"I was minding my own business, as usual," Brittany protested. "Which is more than I can say for you."

"Never mind that, Brittany Tate, tell us where Nikki is!" Robin looked as though she were about to kill the girl.

"Oh, wouldn't you love to know," Brittany purred. Then she snickered softly.

Nancy stepped up to her. She looked Brittany right in the eye, throwing her off balance. "Yes, Brittany, we do want to know. And I want you to tell us *right now*. If you don't, I'll personally hold you responsible for any trouble."

Brittany's jaw dropped open. "You're Nancy Drew, aren't you?"

"Yes, now where's Nikki?" Nancy demanded.

Brittany frowned and puckered her lips. "Okay, okay," she said, backing down. "She went with Dan for a ride in his car. I heard him begging her to go, and she said yes."

"When?" Robin asked breathlessly.

"Oh," Brittany drawled, "just a few minutes ago. Hey, where are you going?"

Nancy, Robin, and Lacey were already halfway around the house on their way to the circular driveway.

"Too late," Nancy groaned when they got there. Dan's car was already gone. "Oh brother," she said under her breath. "I don't like this. I don't like this one bit."

Dejected, the three girls headed back to the Pratts' front door.

"Where could they have gone?" Nancy asked Robin and Lacey as they stood on the steps. "Do they have a special place where they used to go?"

"Not that I know of," Robin answered.

"Sometimes they went to the mall, but it's closed by now," added Lacey.

Jay was standing alone in the doorway as a light rain began to fall. "Hi, beautiful, it's me again," he said to Nancy with a smile. "Ready for that dance now?"

"Jay," Nancy said, "did you see Nikki Masters leave with Dan Taylor?"

"I'm afraid so," Jay nodded, making a face. "How she can go out with him when I'm available is more than I can figure out."

"Jay, this is serious," Nancy told him, facing him squarely. "Did Nikki say anything to you, or anybody, before she left?"

Jay thought about it, and then began his answer with a shrug. "Well, only that she'd be back in a little while."

"She didn't say where they were going?"

"Nope."

Nancy drew in a long breath. Her heart was pounding like crazy, but she knew that getting in her car and searching the streets for Dan and Nikki was foolish. There was no way she could find them without a lead. Besides, she didn't want to risk missing them when—and if—Nikki got back to the party.

"Well," Nancy told Robin and Lacey, "we can only hope she knows what she's doing."

"If she knew what she was doing, then why did she do it?" Lacey asked.

"Yeah," Robin agreed. "Why?"

Nancy thought for a moment. "Nikki's not stupid," she concluded. "If Dan seemed dangerous, she wouldn't have gone with him."

"Sure," Robin said. "But people who are dangerous don't always seem to be, right?"

"Right," Nancy agreed with a shudder. "Well,

there's nothing we can do now but wait. Let's go back inside."

It rained for the next half hour. When Jeremy Pratt came in, he was soaking wet and carrying two huge bags of soda cans. The bags broke the minute he stepped inside the house. Nancy watched as his friends picked up, laughing hysterically the whole time. Jeremy was laughing, too, until Brittany told him Dan Taylor had been at his party.

"What?" Jeremy exploded. "That freak! What a turkey! If that lowlife dares to set foot in my house again, I'm personally going to give him a lesson in manners he'll never forget!"

A crowd had gathered round, enjoying Jeremy's high-humored fury. Jeremy played to the crowd like a born comic.

"Tell me honestly, would anybody at this party ever miss Dan Taylor if, say, he suddenly disappeared? I know I wouldn't!"

Nancy watched it all, detached. "Is Jeremy always like this?" she whispered in Lacey's ear.

"Only when he's angry," Lacey told her. "He gets kind of vicious."

"I'd sure hate to have him mad at me," Nancy remarked.

Nancy looked at her watch a little while later. 11:00. Nikki had been gone over an hour. Nancy was wondering where Nikki could be when a commotion broke out at the front door.

"It's Nikki!" Nancy heard a girl say.

"Excuse me," Nancy said quickly and edged her way over to the door. Then she stopped in her tracks.

Nikki Masters stood there, her hands and face covered with scratches, her shoes muddy, and her clothes soaked and torn. There was a huge rip in the sleeve of her blouse.

"Nikki!" Lacey gasped, running to her. "What in the world happened to you?"

With a wild expression on her delicate face, Nikki turned toward her friend and reached out for support. Then all the blood left her face, and she sank to the floor, lifeless.

Chapter

Eleven

"EVERYBODY STAND BACK! Give her some air." Nancy quickly and firmly took command of the situation. When the chaos died down, Nancy, together with Robin and Lacey, set about reviving Nikki.

After a few moments and a splash of cold water, which Nancy had asked for, Nikki came to and let herself be propped up.

The room was dead silent. Nikki looked around fearfully, then turned to her friends. She buried her head in her hands, and soon great big heaving sobs were coming out of her in waves. Nancy knelt behind her, holding her, while Lacey and Robin crouched by her shoulders.

"Come on, let's get you someplace private," Nancy told her. She turned to the crowd. "The rest of you might as well get back to the party."

Robin and Lacey lifted Nikki up and helped her walk into a study off the main living room. Nancy closed the door so they could have some privacy.

Nikki sat down on the sofa. She was just starting to get her breath back and become calm enough to speak.

"Oh, Nikki," Robin moaned, touching her friend's hair lightly. "Are you hurt?"

"No, not really," Nikki answered weakly.

"Are you sure?" Lacey demanded. There was fire in her eyes, and her lips were pressed together.

Nikki shook her head. "Honestly, I'm okay. It's just, oh, it was so horrible." Nikki burst out in sobs again.

Nancy knelt in front of her and put a comforting hand on her arm. "Nikki," she said softly. "You've got to tell us what happened. From the beginning."

"Okay," said Nikki with a nod and brushed away her tears. "Well, Dan showed up here at the party, you know that. I was in total shock when I saw him."

"Me, too!" Lacey exclaimed. "What nerve he's got!"

"Shhh!" Robin said. "Let Nikki tell us what happened."

"Well, he said he wanted to talk to me, and what could I say? Everyone was staring at us. I think most of them were hoping I'd throw a fit and humiliate him in public, but I would never do that to Dan. Even if he's not my boyfriend, I still care about him."

Nikki was trembling. Nancy quickly took off her sweater and threw it over her friend's shoulders. "Then what happened?" she asked gently.

"Well, we went out into the backyard, and it was okay. Really. He was much more reasonable than I'd seen him in a long time. He said he realized he was acting pretty crazed lately, and he was sorry for upsetting me and all."

"Then what happened?" Lacey prodded.

Nikki smiled weakly at her friend. "Then I told him again that it was definitely over. That we could be friends, from a distance, but that it could never be the way it had been."

"He must have hated hearing that," Robin murmured.

"Well, he didn't argue," Nikki replied. "He just nodded, and I thought maybe this time I'd really gotten through to him. I thought maybe everything was going to be all right."

"Where were you at this point?" Nancy asked. "Were you still here at the party?"

"Yes," Nikki answered. "We were out back under a big tree, in the dark. Dan was sort of staring out into the darkness. He didn't say

93

much. Then, all of a sudden, he asked me to go for a ride with him. To talk some more, he said."

"And you agreed?" Lacey asked, a shocked expression on her face.

"Yes, I did," Nikki said, pausing for a moment. "Could I have a glass of water?" she asked. "My throat feels kind of dry."

"I'll get it." Robin leapt up and went to the door. When she opened it, Nancy could see a bunch of kids huddled around it, whispering furiously. The whispering stopped the second Robin looked outside. "Somebody bring a glass of water," she announced.

"And a wet washcloth, too," Nancy called out.

Robin closed the door and came back to the sofa. "Why can't people mind their own stupid business," she groaned.

"Yeah, it didn't take them long, did it?" Lacey said with a scowl. "Between Brittany and Jeremy, they could put out a real gossip rag. Oh. Sorry, Nikki." Lacey suddenly realized the effect her words must have had on her friend.

Nikki's face was a mask of fear. "Oh, no," she gasped. "They'll take me apart, won't they? Everybody is going to be talking about me now." Her red-rimmed eyes grew sad and distant.

The door opened, and Jay handed the water and washcloth to Robin. The crowd was still out there, still whispering.

"Go on with the story, Nikki," Nancy instructed her. "You were saying he asked you to go for a drive—"

Nikki coughed, took a long drink, and then went on. "I asked him why he wanted to go for a ride, and he kept saying there was something he had to do. He wouldn't say what. I figured he had an errand to run or something. But he was acting awfully nervous again."

"You must have been getting scared by now," Lacey said, her eyes wide.

"Not until he pulled off the road into the woods," Nikki said.

"Where were you by now?" Nancy asked.

Nikki shook her head. "I wasn't really watching the road, but I think we were near the country club. Dan turned off the car, and I wondered what I'd done, you know?" Nikki took a deep breath. "Then he took out that envelope again," she said, staring at the far wall.

"The same one he asked you to take before?" Nancy asked.

Nikki looked at Nancy and nodded. "Same one. He was shaking, and his eyes—you should have seen his eyes—they were wild. It was like we had never had that talk in Jeremy's backyard." Nikki had started to tremble all over.

"Did you take it?" Robin wanted to know.

"No, I didn't want to, but he tried to stuff it into my purse."

The phone next to the sofa rang, startling them

all. Nikki gave a little shriek and jumped up. Then somebody picked up the call in another room, and the phone was quiet.

"Go on, Nikki," Nancy prompted her.

"I tried to run, but he grabbed me," Nikki said. "He was trying to keep me there. I got really scared and I scratched him, I think, but finally I got away. I left my purse there. The navy blue one. He's still got it, I guess.

"I kept running and running, and I fell into some thorns. You can see what a mess I am. Anyway, I found the road finally, and I walked all the way here. I guess that's everything."

The door opened. "Oh, Lacey," Brittany called out, poking her head in the door. "That was your mother on the phone. She wants her little baby to come home. It's eleven-fifteen, you know. Time for beddie-bye."

Lacey reddened with rage at the roar of laughter which followed. "I scratched my mom's car last month," she explained, embarrassed. "Now I've got this dumb curfew."

"We might as well all leave," Nancy said. She turned to Nikki. "Do you feel well enough to go?"

Nikki nodded her head slowly. "I think so."

"Come on, then. I'll drive you home. All of you. This party's over for us."

The four girls walked out of the study through the curious crowd. Nikki kept her head down until they were safely out of the house, in Nancy's car, and out of the driveway.

"Whew!" Lacey sighed in relief as she flicked her red braid over her shoulder. "That was awful. Are you okay, Nikki?"

"I'm okay," Nikki answered, with a shudder. "But I wish Brittany hadn't been there tonight."

"I know. She's such a jerk," Robin muttered, still hot with fury.

Nancy looked over at Nikki. If Brittany had had such a field day with Lacey's curfew, what would she do with Nikki's little adventure?

Nancy dropped Robin and Lacey off, then headed for home. "Nikki," she said as they pulled onto their block, "did anything else happen out there when you were with Dan? Anything you forgot to tell us?" Nancy wanted to have it out with Dan Taylor, and she needed to know every detail.

Nikki looked at Nancy in surprise. "No. Why do you ask?" she asked, cocking her head to one side. "Don't you trust me?"

"Of course I trust you," Nancy told her. "I just wanted to make sure I was totally filled in, that's all. Listen, you get some rest, and put yourself back together. I'll come over for breakfast in the morning."

Nikki smiled with relief. "Great. Nancy, you've been wonderful to me. You've been a true friend, and I really appreciate it. I doubt I'm going to hear from Dan again. I think it's finally all over, thank goodness."

"See you in the morning, Nikki," Nancy said as she pulled up in front of the Masterses' home.

"Aren't you going to park?"

"No, I have a few things I want to check out first," Nancy told her.

Nikki looked curious but seemed to think better of asking too much. "Okay, Nancy. See you tomorrow."

After Nikki got out of the car, Nancy drove off. She wanted to drive past the country club. Maybe Dan was still hanging out near there. If he wasn't, she could still get a look at the area. She'd do some hunting to try to find Nikki's purse, and that envelope Dan had been trying to give her.

About a hundred yards from the club entrance there was a small dirt road leading off the highway. Nancy turned down it, her high beams bouncing off the dense forest growth.

As Nancy drove deeper into the woods, a light caught her eye. A flashing red light. And then another. Coming around a bend, she saw two police cars and an ambulance.

Her heart pounding, she pulled up and got out of the car. She ran over to the nearest police officer. "What's happened?" she asked. "What's going on?"

The policeman turned and shone his flashlight on her. It was Officer Nolan, whom she'd known for years. "Oh, hi, Nancy," he said, in a quiet voice. "I'm afraid it's a murder and a pretty brutal one, too. That's the guy's car."

Nancy's heart leapt into her throat when the policeman turned and flashed his light along the car. Nancy swallowed hard. The car he was pointing to was Dan Taylor's!

Chapter

Twelve

SUDDENLY DIZZY, Nancy leaned back against her Mustang. Distant sirens felt as if they were sounding right in her head, and the flashers wound around crazily in their own wild rhythm. Nancy saw two orderlies loading a stretcher into the ambulance. She looked up but felt too weak to do anything at all.

"I'll go tell the chief you're here," Nolan said, heading off in the direction of the police cars. Nancy tried to shake it off, but a horrible thought kept pounding in her head—I should have seen this coming.

The signs had been there: Dan's growing desperation, the way he kept after Nikki, the way he tried to give her that envelope, the beating he got from Max Hudson. Obviously, Dan had been in greater and greater danger.

He was dead now, Nancy thought with a shudder. And whatever he knew was gone, too.

"Well, if it isn't Nancy Drew!" The voice startled Nancy and brought her back to reality. Looking up, she saw Brenda Carlton from *Today's Times,* one of River Heights's newspapers. Brenda was not one of Nancy's favorite people. She had a good nose for a story, but she always featured its most sensational elements.

"Hello, Brenda," Nancy said wearily.

"So? What are you doing here? Do you know something I don't know but should?" Brenda asked.

"Oh, I just sort of stumbled into this," Nancy said. The excuse sounded lame even to her.

"Right. And I'm the queen of Sheba. Come on, Drew, you know I'm going to find out, with you or without you. So what's your angle on Dan Taylor? He was dating your neighbor Nikki Masters, wasn't he? I heard she gave him a real hard time."

Nancy shuddered. "Brenda, why don't you ever cover *real* news?"

"Is that a hint?" Brenda said with a sneer. "Oh, I get it. All right, I'll find out some other way. But just remember, when you need help from me, you can count on zilch."

Sulking, Brenda turned away from Nancy and

moved off to question a police officer. When she saw Chief McGinnis walking up to Nancy, however, she turned in her tracks. She obviously wanted to be within earshot.

"Hello, Nancy," the chief said, shooting her a grim smile. "Say, you don't look so good. You know this Taylor guy?"

"Not well," Nancy replied sadly. "He had a bad reputation. But I don't think he was a bad kid, Chief—just mixed up. Maybe he got in with the wrong crowd."

Brenda was standing nearby, scribbling furiously. Nancy detected an evil little grin on that self-satisfied face of hers.

"Sounds like you know quite a bit," the chief said, arching his eyebrows. "What do you say we go back to the station together and er"— he looked over at Brenda—"talk about it in private? I'm about done here."

"I've got my car," Nancy offered. "Want to ride with me?"

"Fine," nodded the chief.

"But give me the tour first, okay?"

Chief McGinnis led Nancy over to Dan's car. Next to it was an outline of the body. Judging from the evidence, the police had found Dan on the ground by the driver's side of the car.

"He was hit on the forehead with a rock," the chief explained. "He must have been putting his

The Suspect Next Door

arm up to ward off the blow, because his watch got smashed. Convenient, anyway, because that gives us an exact time of death: ten-fourteen p.m."

Ten-fourteen? Nikki had been with Dan at 10:14!

"We think we know the killer," McGinnis added. "She left a dark blue bag behind."

Nancy's heart sank even farther. This couldn't be happening! Then it hit her—the envelope! It would be inside the purse. "Could I see it?" Nancy asked.

"It's over at headquarters. When we get there, I'll have them take it out of evidence for you." Chief McGinnis was being friendly as always, but Nancy couldn't possibly manage a smile.

The handbag had to be Nikki's. In addition to the time on Dan's watch, the purse made for some pretty serious evidence.

Nancy shivered. She'd just been with Nikki, and Nikki hadn't acted at all like a girl who'd just killed her boyfriend.

And yet, Nancy remembered, Nikki had once told Dan that she'd kill him. She couldn't have really meant it. Or could she?

"I think I know the girl you mean, Chief," Nancy told the officer. "And she's not a killer."

"Well, we'll see about that," he replied.

Nancy took a deep breath and blew it out.

"Okay, let's go," she said huskily. "I've seen enough."

On the trip to the police station Nancy shared everything she knew about the thefts at Vanities and about Dan's relationship with Nikki Masters. Nancy hesitated for a moment, then told him about the envelope and her suspicions about Dan and the missing merchandise.

"I'm telling you, it can't be her, Chief. I've known Nikki forever! The Vanities angle—that's where you'll find the true killer," Nancy said as she accompanied the chief into his office at police headquarters. "Dan worked at Vanities and was fired for lying. I'll bet you anything we'll find a connection there."

Chief McGinnis listened politely, as he always did, but he seemed less than convinced. "You know, Nancy, I have enormous respect for your judgment. I always have."

He started pacing the room, looking uncomfortable with what he had to say. "But this one seems airtight. Taylor is seen leaving this party with the girl at ten. She comes back at eleven, all scratched and mussed. She admits they struggled. Then we find the guy. His watch is smashed at ten-fourteen. Her bag is on the seat. He's lying next to the car, with the rock that smashed his head lying next to him. I'll lay you odds her prints are all over the inside of the car. Can you see what I'm thinking?"

"Are you going to arrest her tonight?" Nancy asked, nervously running her hand through her hair. Obviously defending Nikki against this barrage of evidence was getting Nancy nowhere.

"That's my plan at the moment. I'm just waiting for my people to get back. You never know," he added. "She might run."

"She won't run, Chief," Nancy assured him. "Because she's innocent. I don't know what happened out there tonight, but I know what didn't happen. Nikki Masters didn't kill Dan Taylor!"

"I wish I could agree, Nancy," Chief McGinnis said, stroking his chin. "But what proof can you give me? Intuition just doesn't cut it in the courts."

Nancy rubbed her temples. "Let me think," she said. "Can I see the bag?" she asked. Chief McGinnis signaled for an officer to get it.

"Here you go," she said in a minute, tossing the bag onto the chief's desk.

It was Nikki's, all right. Nancy recognized it right away. She picked up the purse and gently unzipped it. Except for some makeup and a purse-size atomizer, it was empty. "There's no envelope," she murmured, half to herself.

"I can see that," the chief acknowledged. "But

that doesn't mean there ever was an envelope. We have only her word for it."

Nancy gritted her teeth in frustration, but she knew Chief McGinnis was right. He had to look at hard evidence—that was his job.

But there *had* been an envelope; Nancy was sure. And if Nikki had killed Dan Taylor, and forgotten her purse, as the chief was saying, the envelope would still be in the purse! Which meant someone *else* had taken it.

There was no way to convince Chief McGinnis that the envelope had existed. Nancy thought hard, trying to come up with other inconsistencies.

"What about the position of the body?" she asked. "If Nikki tried to get out the passenger side, and he tried to stop her, his body would be sprawled across the front seat, not outside on the driver's side."

"Go on, I'm listening," the chief said, stretching out in his chair and putting his feet up on his desk. "Of course," he added, "you're assuming it happened just as she told you it did. You told me she said they argued. And you know that in an argument, we get a little hot sometimes and forget the odd detail."

"Yes, they argued," Nancy shot back, getting up and pacing the room, "but the place he took her might not have been the exact same place he was found. He might have met up with somebody afterward. If he was in on the thefts at Vanities, he might have been meeting his partner in crime."

"You're forgetting the watch," the chief pointed out. "He was with her at ten-fourteen, wasn't he?"

Nancy slumped in defeat. How could she argue with that hard fact? "I guess so," she admitted. "But, Chief, couldn't you give me just a little more time to sniff things out? A day, maybe two? I might come up with something concrete. Think what it would do to that poor girl to be arrested like that."

"Assuming she's innocent," Chief McGinnis said.

"Assuming she's innocent," Nancy echoed.

"Well, maybe I could give you a day," he mused, fingering some papers on his desk. "But no more."

Nancy straightened up, every instinct alert. She had twenty-four hours. One precious day to get Nikki out of the worst jam of her entire life.

There was a knock on the door, and an officer poked his head through. "Chief, we found something written in the dirt," he said. "Looks like our boy wrote it with his fingernail before he died."

Chief McGinnis sat up quickly. "What was it? Got a picture?" he demanded.

"Sure do," the officer replied, spreading a large photo out on the desk. "The people at the lab just got through with it. It's just one letter. Any idea what it stands for?"

"I'm afraid I do," the chief said slowly as he stared at the photo.

Nancy craned her neck to get a look, too. Etched in the dirt beside the outline of Dan's body was the letter *N!*

Chapter

Thirteen

Nancy stared hard at Chief McGinnis. She could tell what he was thinking. If it stood for Nikki, that one letter—*N*—was hard and solid evidence.

"I'm sorry, Nancy. I have no choice," he said gently. "I understand how you feel, but I've got to consider the evidence against Nikki Masters. Tomorrow morning, we're going to call her in for questioning, and even if she tells us the same story she told you, we may have to arrest her. You might as well go home and get a good night's sleep."

Defeated, Nancy said good night and stepped

out into the late summer night. The chief was right about one thing. There was nothing she could do for Nikki that night.

The next morning Nancy got up before seven. She dressed quickly, wanting to get to Nikki's house before the police did. Then at least Nikki and her family would get the bad news from a friend, not a stranger.

"Nancy, come in." An ashen-faced Mr. Masters opened the door and greeted Nancy with barely a nod. He ran a hand through his faded blond hair. "She's in the dining room."

Nancy heard sobbing coming from inside. Following Mr. Masters, she found the family grouped around the dining room table.

Today's Times lay on the table before them. Its huge headline shouted "Local Boy Murdered. Police Seek Girlfriend for Questioning." Nancy had beaten the police to the Masterses' home, but Brenda Carlton had managed to cross the finish line first.

"Nancy!" Nikki's slender shoulders were shivering, and her voice was weak from crying. Her mother had a comforting arm around her.

"Hello, Nancy." Nikki's mom turned her tear-stained face in Nancy's direction. Her hazel eyes were full of sorrow. "Have you seen the morning paper?"

"Take a look." Nikki's father pointed to the *Times* with a look of shocked confusion. "Can you believe it? According to this, Nikki has already been tried and convicted!"

"I'm so sorry," Nancy said, going over to them and putting a hand on Nikki's shoulder. "It's awful, I know. But Nikki's going to come through this. She's innocent, and everyone's going to find that out."

Nikki bit her knuckles and stifled a sob. "Oh, Nancy," she said. "What if I'm not innocent? What if I really did it? I mean, what if I blacked out or something?"

"You didn't black out," Nancy told her firmly. "And you didn't kill him. The police just want to see you for questioning, that's all."

"But the article says he was killed at ten-fourteen! I was with him at ten-fourteen, Nancy!" Nikki said with a gulp.

Nancy ignored that remark. There had to be an explanation about the time, and she'd find it. "Nikki," she began gently. "There are things I didn't tell you about Dan."

Nikki and her parents fell silent. Nancy went on. "At the time I didn't want to upset you, or scare you. But I'm pretty sure Dan was involved in a series of robberies I've been investigating at a store in the mall called Vanities."

Nikki's father seemed to come back to life. "You mean you think Dan was in on them?" he asked grimly.

"Yes. And I don't think he was working alone, either," Nancy replied firmly.

"Well, if he was involved with criminals . . ." Mr. Masters murmured.

"One of his partners might have killed him," Nancy finished for him. "I've told the police about it. Right now, unfortunately, I don't have any hard evidence."

"The article says that Nikki's handbag was found at the scene of the crime," said Mrs. Masters, with a quiver in her voice.

Nancy turned to Nikki. "The envelope, Nikki. Are you sure you put it in the bag? Because we couldn't find it last night."

"Yes! I'm sure! Dan stuffed it in!" Nikki cried.

"That means somebody took it," Nancy said. "There must have been important evidence in that envelope. I suspect it was about the robberies."

"Wait, Nancy," Nikki said. "Slow down a minute. Are you sure Dan really was a thief? I knew him pretty well. Well enough to know he was basically an honest person. Maybe he took something that wasn't his once, but I can't imagine him organizing a series of robberies. That doesn't sound like Dan."

"Can you be sure?" Nancy asked, trying to be gentle. "How well did you really know him, Nikki? You know he lied, that he was fired from his job. And you know he was giving you things he couldn't afford to buy."

Releasing herself from her mother's embrace, Nikki fell back in her chair. "He would disappear for a day or two sometimes. And when he'd come back, he always brought a gift. But he'd never say where he'd been. Just 'away,' making 'big deals.'"

Nancy felt like kicking herself. If she'd only told Nikki about Dan and the thefts earlier, she might have learned a lot, maybe even prevented his death.

"Do you have a lawyer?" Nancy asked, turning to Nikki's parents.

"We know a very good lawyer," Mrs. Masters said with a weary grin. "Your father."

"We're hoping Carson will help us," Mr. Masters continued.

"I'm sure he will. He's due back from Chicago later today. I'll leave a note for him to call you."

"Thanks, Nancy," Mrs. Masters said gratefully.

"Nikki, don't say anything to the police until you talk to my dad," Nancy advised, giving her friend a comforting pat on the shoulder.

"Won't that make me look even more guilty?" Nikki asked.

"No," Nancy answered simply. "It's called constitutional rights. The chief will understand."

"I hear a car," Mrs. Masters said ominously.

Stepping to the window, Nancy saw a River Heights patrol car quietly pull up to the house. The lack of flashers and sirens showed that the chief was being sensitive to the situation at least.

"Oh, no," Nikki moaned as she walked over to

the window and peered out. There was a look of sheer terror in her eyes as she watched the officers walk toward the house.

Nancy turned to her. "You're innocent, Nikki, just keep remembering that. And while you're at the station house, remember, I'm going to be out tracking down the real killer."

The doorbell rang, and Nikki shuddered. Shooting his daughter a grim look, Mr. Masters opened the door and spoke quietly with the officers. "She'll be right with you," he told them finally.

Mr. Masters bit his lip. "I tried to convince them to let us come with you, but they said they want to question you alone. Apparently we're not to come along."

Mrs. Masters held back a sob. Nikki took a deep breath. "Thanks, Nancy," she said softly. She hugged her parents and told them she loved them. Then she stepped out the door.

"I'll leave you two alone," Nancy said quietly as the shattered parents watched their daughter step into the police car. Mr. and Mrs. Masters could only nod.

Nancy slipped out of the house and hurried home. She went straight to her father's study where she left a note for him about Nikki. Then she picked up her purse. She was just about to leave her house when the phone rang.

"Hello," Nancy said.

"You're home," came Ned's gentle voice on the other end. "I was a little worried about you when you didn't show up last night."

"Ned!" said Nancy, with a gasp. She'd completely forgotten about him. "Our stakeout!"

"I was there," Ned said calmly. "Where were you?"

"Oh, Ned, you're not going to believe what happened. I take it you haven't read a newspaper this morning."

"No," he said cautiously. "Should I have?"

"Dan Taylor was murdered."

"Wow," Ned said after a moment's silence.

"And the police think Nikki did it!"

Ned let out a low whistle. "That's intense," he murmured. "I guess that means you've got a whole new case."

"It looks that way. I've got to try to clear Nikki." Nancy paused. "Did anything happen at Vanities?" she asked.

"Nope. I did try to call you, by the way, but Hannah said you were out. So I figured I'd better stick around and hope you showed up."

"Oh, Ned! I'm sorry."

"Hey, no apologies necessary. You had other things to worry about. So tell me, where do you go from here? And how can I help?" Ned asked.

"You're such a sweetheart," Nancy told him.

"I like hearing that on our anniversary," said Ned.

THE NANCY DREW FILES

"Oh! Our anniversary!" said Nancy with a gasp. She wasn't about to add, "I forgot," though in fact, she had.

"It's okay," Ned said. "I know you love me, in spite of the evidence. Happy anniversary, Nancy."

"Oh, I love you so much," Nancy murmured. "Happy anniversary to you, too, Ned. I wish we could celebrate, but—"

"Don't worry, we'll celebrate soon," Ned said.

"Meanwhile, I may need you on this case," Nancy said. "Can I call you later?"

"You can always call me, Nancy. You know that," he replied.

"Thanks, Ned." She hung up and left the house. She wanted to find out more about Jeremy Pratt. Jeremy hated Dan. He made a show of his dislike at his party. And he'd been gone from his own party for a part of the evening.

Nancy drove to the Pratts', where the housekeeper told her that Jeremy was playing his weekly round of golf at the country club.

More determined than ever, Nancy headed for the country club. She shivered again at the thought of what had happened the night before. She just *had* to clear Nikki Masters.

Nancy caught up with Jeremy on the fifth hole. He had just hit a long drive down the fairway and he seemed terribly pleased with himself.

"Hello, there," he called out breezily when he

116

noticed Nancy rushing up to him. "Do I know you?"

"I'm Nancy Drew. I was at your party last night," she answered.

"That's right, someone said you're a detective. Wild, isn't it?"

"So you've heard?"

"Who hasn't? You can't miss the police. They're everywhere! It happened right over near the fifteenth tee. Frankly, I can't say I'm broken up about Dan, but poor Nikki," he said with a shake of his head.

"I guess he provoked her into it," Jeremy went on for Nancy's benefit. "The way he was always following her everywhere, like a sick little puppy."

"Excuse me, Jeremy," Nancy interrupted. "But where were you at the time of the murder?"

Jeremy put his club in his bag. "You think I killed Dan Taylor?" he said with a sneer. "Get real. Besides, I have an alibi. I was back at the party by ten. Check with Brittany. She'll tell you the same thing."

With a bored shrug, Jeremy hopped onto his electric golf cart. "Need a lift?" he asked with a nasty grin.

"No, thanks," Nancy answered icily.

"Well, then, I'm off!" he announced as he rode away toward his ball.

Nancy checked her watch. It was early, just

nine-fifteen. Vanities wouldn't open for another forty-five minutes.

Since she had time, Nancy decided to check on Nikki at the station house. She found Chief McGinnis in his office.

"Nancy!" he said in surprise, looking up at her.

"I came to see how Nikki's doing," she told him.

"We've just finished questioning her," he said. "But when your dad gets back, we'll want her down here again. Nice girl," he added, thoughtfully. "It's a shame."

"If it's okay, I'd like to drive her back home," Nancy offered.

"Sure," he answered. "She's in Room one hundred three."

Nancy gave the chief a little wave and headed off to find her. Nikki was alone in a colorless office, looking lonely and frightened.

"Nancy!" she said, brightening a little when Nancy poked her head in the door.

"Come on," said Nancy. "Let's get you out of here. You look like you could use a little fresh air."

Nikki blinked at the strong sunlight as they stepped out onto the steps. Down below on the street, a car drove by, with a group of teens inside.

Nikki waved weakly to them, obviously recognizing them as schoolmates.

But they didn't wave back. They just stared at

her. The girl who was driving slowed down. Another girl leaned out the window, her face set in an ugly sneer. She shot Nikki a look of pure hatred and screamed loud enough for everyone around to hear:

"Murderer!"

Chapter
Fourteen

THE CAR PASSED BY, and Nikki stood on the steps, frozen. "I just realized the most horrible thing," she gasped.

"What's that?" Nancy asked.

"This is never going to end. Even if they find me innocent, the rumors will never die." Nikki's red eyes began to swim again with tears. "Oh, Nancy, what am I going to do?"

Giving her friend false assurance now wouldn't help her in the end, Nancy thought. Instead, she held Nikki by the shoulders and gave her a comforting smile. "Other people have lived through it, Nikki, and you will, too. One thing about this whole ordeal, it'll separate your true friends from pretenders."

"Probably you, Robin, and Lacey will be the only ones who will still talk to me when this is over." Nikki's head hung down and she wiped the tears from her eyes.

"I don't believe that, Nikki. There are other good people out there. You'll find them."

Nancy bundled Nikki into the Mustang and drove her home.

Nikki's parents were anxiously waiting for her. "She's free, for now," Nancy told them. "They want to see her again when my dad gets back." Nancy left Nikki in their care and drove off toward Vanities.

By the time she got there, it was almost eleven, and the store was starting to get crowded with Saturday shoppers.

"Nancy!" Trisha waved and came over to greet her from across the store. "Long time no see," she said with a smile. For some reason, Trisha seemed much friendlier than the last time Nancy had seen her.

"Where's Charlene?" Nancy wanted to know, looking at the vacant spot behind the cash register.

"Out sick," Trisha told her. "If you believe her excuses."

"Dan Taylor was murdered last night," Nancy said. "Did you know?"

Trisha's face took on a serious expression. She shook her head sadly. "Yes, I read about it in the papers. They said his girlfriend did it."

Just the thought of Brenda writing that story made Nancy's blood boil, but she couldn't let her feelings get the better of her now. "Is Max around? I want to ask him a few questions."

Trisha's eyes widened. "You think he's the thief?" she whispered. "Really? I don't think he's smart enough."

"I just want to talk to him." On a hunch, Nancy said, "Oh, by the way, Trisha, I hear you and Dan were rather friendly at one time."

Trisha gasped. "Well, I wouldn't go that far," she said with an edge to her voice. "He was really a nice kid underneath all the bluster. I felt sorry for him—he had so many big dreams," Trisha said sadly. "He was always telling me how he was going to be a millionaire by the time he was thirty." She let out a little laugh.

Nancy ignored Trisha's malicious joke. "By the way, I'm checking up on where everyone was last night, in case there's a connection between Dan's death and the store thefts."

Trisha looked startled. "What are you talking about?" she exclaimed. "His girlfriend did it. If you're accusing me, you might as well know I was with Kate Hayes at a dinner with clients from L.A., and we were there until eleven. You can check it out if you want."

"Just looking at all the angles," Nancy explained.

"Max is in the back," Trisha said coldly.

Nancy walked through the boutique to the stockroom. Max Hudson was at work, opening cartons.

"Max, I'm asking everyone the same question. Where were you last night?"

"None of your business!" he snapped angrily.

"Max, let me level with you," Nancy began delicately. "A few nights ago I saw you at the Sixplex, and then later, at the River Heights Arcade, I saw Dan getting beat up—"

"Okay, okay," Max said, tucking the utility knife into his shirt pocket and facing her. "So you saw me punching out Dan Taylor."

"That's right," Nancy answered. "Why?"

Max looked scared. Then, he exploded. "That turkey owed me money! That's why. I've been trying to get it back for months, and finally I blew my cool. I got tired of all his excuses about why he didn't have the money."

"How much money did he owe you?" Nancy asked.

"Two hundred bucks," the stockboy complained. "But, hey, I didn't kill the guy. I'm not so hard up I'd kill somebody for two hundred dollars."

Taking the knife from his pocket, he went back to work.

Nancy had to admit Max's point about two hundred dollars not being worth killing for. But *if* Max and Dan had been partners in the Vanities thefts, there could have been a lot more than two hundred dollars at stake. Nancy resolved to keep her eye on Max Hudson.

Nancy left Vanities, went to a phone booth on the mall's street level, and dialed Nikki's number. She'd reached a dead end at Vanities, but maybe the girl could remember some small clue that would provide Nancy with a lead. True, there was a phone in Kate Hayes's office, but Nancy didn't want anybody else listening in on her conversation.

"She's feeling better now," Mr. Masters replied to Nancy's question about how Nikki was. "Do you want to talk to her?"

"Please," said Nancy.

Nikki got right on the line. "Hello, Nancy? I really haven't gotten a chance to say thank you for all your help, and I don't know when I will again."

"Don't mention it," Nancy said. "Nikki, about last night. I'm kind of at an impasse. Could you just go over it one more time for me? Any little thing might help."

"Well," said Nikki, sounding calm and rational now, "as I told you, Dan was very apologetic, and said if I wanted out, that was okay, but that he'd made a decision, and he was turning over a new leaf."

"He used those words? 'Turning over a new leaf'?"

"Well, something like that. I got the impression he was willing to say goodbye, if I would only spend this one last night keeping him company. When he asked me to take a ride with him, that's what I thought was up."

"Go on," Nancy prompted.

"It started to rain, I remember, because he turned on the windshield wipers. Then he pulled up at a store and went in to get sodas."

"You didn't mention that before," Nancy said, alert.

"Didn't I? Well, he went in for the sodas, and he made a phone call. I could see him through the store window."

"A phone call? He made a phone call?"

"Yes. I didn't ask him who he was talking to, though. I mean, I'm trying to ease myself out of this guy's life, right? So I wasn't going to ask him about anything."

Nancy nodded. "Okay, okay. Go on."

The rest of the story was the same as before.

"That phone call," Nancy said when Nikki had finished. "Is there anything else about it you can remember?"

"Well, let's see," Nikki said, pausing. "No, not really, except that it looked like a pretty intense conversation."

"Oh? How could you tell?"

"Well, he was gesturing with his arm, and

every once in a while he'd rub his forehead like he was frustrated."

"Thanks, Nikki," Nancy said. "You've been a big help, believe it or not."

"I have?"

"Yes, you have. Nikki, I've got to go now, but I'll call you later."

After Nancy hung up, she stood in the phone booth for a full five minutes. Dan had made a phone call. Why, at a time like that, in the middle of a crisis with the girl he loved, would he have taken time out to call somebody?

It had to have been an important phone call. But what could have been so pressing on a rainy Saturday night? Dan had mentioned turning over a new leaf. Could he have been calling his partner in the Vanities crimes? Arranging a meeting? Maybe Nikki's pleading with Dan had had some effect after all! Maybe Dan was telling his partner that he wanted out. And maybe his partner had killed him because of it!

Buzzing with excitement, Nancy raced to her car and drove straight to police headquarters. She wasn't quite ready to confront Chief McGinnis with her fleshed-out theory, but she wanted to have a look at the official reports on the case. They'd be a lot more complete now than they were late last night.

"Still working on my theory," she explained to

Chief McGinnis when he gave her a puzzled look. "Mind if I mess up your desk?"

The chief laughed out loud at that one. His desk could not have been more of a mess than it already was. "How are the Masterses doing?" he asked.

"Not too bad, considering. My dad'll be back this afternoon, I think. He'll want to get the whole story from Nikki."

"I'll be seeing him tonight, then, I guess," he said, wearily rubbing a hand over his face. "Guess I'd better go home and catch forty winks. I've been up most of the night," he said, throwing her a smile. "Whatever you do, don't 'clean up' my desk, understand? I've got my own unique sort of order, believe it or not."

"Oh, I believe it." Nancy laughed, sitting down in his chair and getting to work.

An hour later she had gotten to the bottom of the pile of evidence. In front of her was the police photo of the letter *N* Dan Taylor had scratched into the ground. She stared at it, thinking. The case was just out of reach, inches beyond her grasp. What was the missing link?

Then she realized what she was looking at. In her musings, Nancy had cocked her head, so that she was now staring down at the *N* from one side. It was a funny-looking *N,* sort of like a lightning bolt.

127

In fact, now that she looked at it, she saw the letter was not an *N* at all. It was a *Z!*

Nancy ran her hands through her hair, tugging at it in frustration. *Z—Z—*What did it mean? None of her suspects' names began with *Z,* and yet, Nancy knew it had to be an important clue. If only she could make the connection.

The day was flying by, and there was a lot more ground to cover. Nancy filed the *Z* question away for the moment and quickly went through what was left of the evidence. There was nothing there. In fact, there was nothing anywhere about the envelope Dan had stuffed in Nikki's purse. The chief thought Nikki was making it up, but Nancy believed—no, she knew—there had been an envelope!

Now it was gone. That meant Dan's killer had taken it. Now, why would the killer take a love letter? Unless . . .

Unless it wasn't a love letter at all. And if it wasn't a love letter, why was Dan giving it to Nikki? There could be only one reason. *To keep someone else from finding it!*

Carson Drew arrived home that afternoon. By the time Nancy had briefed him, taken him over to the Masterses', and left him in charge, it was nearly five. She barely made it to Vanities in time to tail Max Hudson.

Max left work, got into an old sports car, and

drove to what was apparently his apartment. It was in an old, run-down building. Nancy sat in her car and waited.

After fifteen minutes Max emerged from the building, dressed in a freshly pressed shirt and slacks. He seemed to walk taller as he headed for his car. Nancy waited until she could follow unnoticed, then she pulled onto the street behind him.

He drove for about fifteen minutes until he came to the border of Riverview Park. There, he slowed down, and suddenly a figure in a raincoat and floppy hat came out of the dark trees and ran to his car.

Nancy's eyes widened in surprise. Could this be it? Had she stumbled onto the big break of the case?

Max and the person he'd picked up drove a few miles out of town to a path by the river. There, they parked and got out of the car.

Nancy doused her headlights and quietly followed them on foot. Her flesh was prickling. Who was the mysterious person Max had picked up?

Dodging from tree to tree, she watched as Max and his companion strolled along. Finally, the mysterious stranger took off his hat, and a cascade of curly hair fell.

There, standing in the twilight next to Max, was Charlene Rice!

Max put his arms out and wrapped them around Charlene's neck. Nancy gasped, and her whole body tensed, poised to leap out from behind the tree to help Charlene.

But as she watched, Nancy saw Max pull Charlene to him. He wrapped his arms around her and overpowered her with a sizzling kiss!

Chapter
Fifteen

STUNNED, NANCY WATCHED as Max and Charlene shared another passionate kiss. In her surprise, she forgot she was hiding and coughed.

Charlene's eyes popped open. Over Max's shoulder, she saw Nancy. Flying backward out of his grasp, Charlene let out a shriek. Max spun around and saw Nancy, too.

Nancy half expected him to walk over and slug her, or chew her out, at least. But instead of anger in his eyes, she saw pure fear.

"Please—" he begged, moving toward her. "Please, don't tell Tony."

"He would be so upset," Charlene echoed,

leaning back against Max's car fender for balance, her eyes fixed on Nancy. "He'd be really angry, too. Tony has a bad temper. I know he'd get Max fired! And there's no telling what he'd do to me."

Nancy stood there dumbfounded. So this was their big secret!

"See, I've been planning on breaking up with Tony for a while. I'm going to do it, too. I am!" Charlene explained. "Max and I just realized recently how we felt about each other. This is it, for both of us. It's like a revelation or something."

It was all Nancy could do not to roll her eyes.

"We had our first date just the other night— when I said I went to that movie. I didn't really see it, by the way," Charlene confessed.

"I knew that," said Nancy. "Were you together last night, too?"

"Yes," Max said. "Sorry I was so rude to you when you asked me, but I couldn't tell you where I really was. Tony was nearby," he explained.

"We were together the whole evening, Nancy," Charlene said. "We went out to Woodmont and hung out at this dance club where nobody knew us."

"But if you ask them at the club, they'll tell you we were there," Max said. "We were a big hit on the dance floor," he added, giving Charlene a smoldering look.

Nancy saw that Charlene was blushing. "With Tony I always felt too self-conscious to dance," the salesgirl said.

"Speaking of Tony," Nancy broke in, "any idea where he was last night?"

"Yes," Charlene replied. "I made sure he was busy before I made plans with Max. Tony was at a big family get-together. You could probably check with one of his cousins. There are dozens of them, and each one is meaner than the next." She giggled a little and gave Max an adoring look.

"Well, I guess that's that." Nancy sighed. "Oh, and don't worry. I won't say a word to anybody."

"Thanks, Nancy," Charlene said sweetly. "This way we can break it to Tony when the time is right." With a wave, Nancy turned and walked away from them.

It seemed to her that everyone had an alibi for the past evening at 10:14. Everyone but Nikki Masters.

Could the killer have deliberately set the watch back after the murder, then smashed it to give a false time? It was possible. Nancy knew that had been done before.

But Nancy didn't think it likely. There had been a struggle, that was for sure. And since Dan had been killed with a rock, the killing more than likely had been unexpected. Only people who plan a murder think to set watches back. People who kill in the heat of an argument don't.

Driving through the dusky early evening toward home, Nancy tried to imagine the moment in question.

Dan is at the scene, and Nikki has just left. Someone else arrives. There's an argument, a struggle, a blow. The killer sees the bag on the seat of the car, with the envelope sticking out. He or she takes it, looks inside, and decides to keep it, leaving the navy purse behind to implicate its owner, whoever she may be.

But what had the argument been about?

Nancy remembered that Dan had told Nikki he wanted to "turn over a new leaf." Assuming that meant he wanted to get out of crime, Dan would have been dangerous to his former partner. Especially if the envelope contained evidence to support his story.

It all made perfect sense! Photos, copies of receipts, anything to implicate his partner in crime. And who better to hold on to it for him than Nikki Masters, the soul of innocence! That must have been why he'd begged her to keep it. It would also explain why he told her she didn't even have to open it!

Nancy's mind was racing. The only problem with her theory was that she couldn't prove any of it. But—if she set the right trap for the right person, she could get the killer to implicate him or herself. There was only one problem: she still didn't know who it was.

Nancy's thoughts went back to that letter Z.

Why had it struck such a chord in her? What was the clue?

Z—Z—Nancy repeated to herself. Of course! Z was the designer's mark on the back of the necklace Dan had given Nikki!

Nancy threw the Mustang into a quick U-turn and headed back for the mall. It was Sunday night and the mall would be closed, but she hoped she could get in through the movie entrance. There was something she needed to check, and there wasn't a moment to lose.

Nancy parked in the farthest row of the mall parking lot and began walking toward the movie theater. As soon as the ticket sellers began talking to each other, she quietly slipped into the mall itself.

Nancy hurried in the direction of Vanities, praying the electronic code hadn't been changed since the last robbery. If it was different, a buzzer would go off, alerting every security guard within a quarter of a mile that she was breaking in.

Nancy got to the electronic lock and punched in the first digit. No buzzer. A wave of relief flooded her. If her luck held out, she'd be in the store within minutes.

A subtle click of the lock told Nancy that she'd succeeded. She reached in her purse for the pocket flashlight on the end of her key ring. The small circle of light was all she needed to find her way to the office.

There, she pulled out ledger after ledger, scanning the purchase records. She wanted to track down where the Z jewelry had come from. If Dan had written that letter in the dirt, it had to be a clue about who his killer was.

Nancy's eyes searched the papers. Then, bingo! Every piece of Z jewelry had come from a single source: Zero's, in *Denver, Colorado!*

What was it about Denver that rang a bell with Nancy? She thought for a moment. Then it came to her. Bess and George had told her that the man in the cowboy hat was from Denver. *And* he was in town the night Dan was killed! *And* he was Trisha Rapp's boyfriend!

To prove her theory further, Nancy flipped through Vanities' employee records. Once she reached the R's and had checked Trisha's out-of-town references, she knew she had found what she was looking for.

Trisha Rapp was from Denver, too.

Chapter
Sixteen

NANCY WAS UP EARLY the next morning. She had a lot of ground to cover that day and the sooner she started the better. First she wanted to stop by the Taylors'.

When Marie Taylor saw Nancy standing in the doorway, she burst into fresh sobs. From the ravaged look on her face and the dark circles under her eyes, Mrs. Taylor looked as if she'd been crying for weeks.

"It's sweet of you to come," Dan's mother managed to say.

"I'm so sorry about Dan." She paused. "Mrs. Taylor, I want to find his killer. Will you help me?"

"What makes you think I can help? I can't! I have no idea who would do something so horrible to my boy!" Dan's mother sobbed.

"Mrs. Taylor, you said Dan traveled for Vanities. Where did he go?"

"I have no idea. Dan didn't tell me very much about his business, and I didn't want to pry," his mother said.

"Well, if I could have a look at Dan's things," Nancy urged gently, "we might learn a lot."

"If you think it'll help, I'll take you to his room." Dan's mother led Nancy through the living room and down a small dark corridor to a closed door.

"This is his room. I'm much too upset to set foot in there right now. But take all the time you need." Dan's mother turned away and headed for the kitchen.

Nancy walked into the room and flicked on the light. An eerie feeling passed over her. The boy whose room this was would never be coming back.

A framed mocked-up headline announced "Dan Taylor Makes First Million." Dan couldn't have known his name would be featured in a real and much grimmer headline.

On the bureau was a framed photo of Dan and Nikki. They looked so relaxed and so happy together. It was obviously from earlier days.

Nancy riffled through the papers in Dan's desk, but nothing there confirmed her theory.

Now, she thought, she'd have to proceed without it.

Defeated, she turned to leave the room. As she did, she noticed the grip of a suitcase sticking out from under the bed.

Dragging it out, she examined the airport tags attached to the handle. DVR. Denver. Another piece of the puzzle fell into place. It couldn't be a coincidence that Dan's "business" took him to Denver.

On her way out Nancy stopped to ask Dan's mother a question. "Mrs. Taylor, you said Dan went on a business trip a few days ago. When was that? Friday?"

"That's right, Friday." The older woman nodded.

"Thank you, Mrs. Taylor. You've been a great help. We're going to find Dan's killer, I promise you."

Leaving the unhappy woman behind, Nancy made her way back to the Masterses' house. She needed Nikki's help with the next phase of her plan. When she got there, she found Nikki in tears.

"I've gotten three crank calls in the last twenty minutes!" she cried miserably. "Finally, I called Robin. I thought, at least she'll talk to me. But her stepfather picked up, and"—Nikki burst into tears again—"and he wouldn't let her get on the line with me! He said he didn't want his daughter being mixed up with a killer!"

"Don't worry, Nikki," Nancy comforted her. "The case is practically solved. I know who the real killer is now."

"You do?" Nikki threw her arms around Nancy's neck. "I knew you'd come through for me."

Nancy smiled. "But I'm going to need your help to set a trap. We're going to put on a little show. You, me, and Ned. And you're going to be the star, Nikki."

Nikki cocked her head to one side. "But I'm not an actress, Nancy," she protested.

"That's all right," Nancy said. "In this show, you'll be playing yourself. Can I use your telephone? I want to call Ned."

Ned picked up the phone after the first ring. "I had a feeling it was you," he told her. "Is this the call I've been waiting for?"

"It sure is, Seargent Nickerson. Can you meet me at the ice-cream parlor in the mall around six-thirty?" she asked.

"Sure," he said.

"And if you wouldn't mind, could you pick up a loaded starter's pistol, and a couple of vials of stage blood? You can get the pistol at a sporting goods store and the Party Store should carry the stage blood."

"That's quite a shopping list. What's going on?"

"I can't tell you right now," Nancy told him. "But be prepared to do some heavy acting."

"Come on, Nan, I can't stand the suspense," he protested.

"Why, Ned, I thought you loved suspense," she said coyly. "See you at six-thirty."

Nancy hung up and felt in her purse for the portable radio/cassette recorder she'd gotten Ned. She'd meant to give it to him on Saturday during their stakeout of Vanities. Now it would be a late anniversary gift. Better late than never, Nancy thought. Meanwhile, the little machine was going to come in handy.

"See you at six-thirty," Nancy said to Nikki as she left. "I'll explain everything then."

At six o'clock Nancy made a brief stop at Vanities. "Charlene," she said, calling her over, "can I talk to you a minute?"

The girl nodded her head, and, despite a stare or two from Trisha, moments later the two of them were in the back of the stockroom. "I need your help," she told the salesgirl. "Max's, too."

"Sure!" gushed the now-grateful Charlene. "You're helping us, so anything we can do."

"I want you and Max to be out of here by five minutes to seven, okay? And you've got to make sure Tony is gone, too. It's very important, understand? I need the three of you out of the way."

"Okay, Nancy," Charlene nodded. "But why? What's up?"

"I can't tell you right now," Nancy said, waving her off. "You'll find out soon enough."

Checking her watch, Nancy headed over to the ice-cream parlor and waited for Ned and Nikki to show up. Ned arrived at precisely 6:30. "How's that for punctuality?" he said, giving her a big smile.

"Oh, Ned, what did I do to deserve you?" Nancy said, leaning over the table and planting a kiss on his lips. "Happy anniversary, Ned." She presented him with the radio/recorder. "Sorry it's not gift wrapped, but you're going to need to use it right away."

"Thanks, Nan," he said, turning it over in his hands. "So what's the plan?"

"Let's wait for Nikki to show up. Then I'll fill you both in on what we've got ahead of us tonight," Nancy said. She reached out for Ned's hand and gave it a squeeze.

Within a few minutes, Nikki came breezing in. "Sorry I'm late," she said, sitting down next to Nancy.

"Do you guys know each other?" Nancy asked.

"We've met once or twice. Hi, Ned," Nikki said. Nancy saw Nikki smile for the first time in days.

"Hi, Nikki, nice to see you," Ned answered.

"Ned's going to be your costar."

"Okay, Nancy," Ned said. "Enough suspense. Which play *is* it that we're going to perform in?"

"It's sort of a melodrama, but if everything turns out right, we'll end up with the proof we need to send Dan's killer away for a long time."

Nancy explained her theory about how Dan Taylor had gotten involved in fencing stolen merchandise for Trisha and her boyfriend in the cowboy hat.

"But we need it on tape—" Nancy pointed to Ned's gift. "That's where my trap comes in."

"So tell us what we have to do," Nikki said.

After coaching Ned and Nikki on their roles, Nancy looked across the mall to Vanities. She saw Max and Charlene leaving, with Tony between them. Good, she thought. They came through.

"Nancy, it's six fifty-five," Ned announced softly.

Nancy nodded. "Let's go," she said.

She led them down a stairway to the loading docks, and then up a ramp to the back door of Vanities.

Nancy's watch read seven o'clock. The store was closing. Everyone would be up front. Nancy pressed the combination and let them all in.

The stockroom was deserted. Ned took the minirecorder out of his jacket pocket, pressed the record button, then slipped it back in. They all took positions behind packing crates to wait.

Seconds later Nancy heard the click of high heels on tile. Trisha Rapp came into view, then disappeared into her office. Nancy could see her through the open door, going over the day's receipts.

Nancy gave Ned a signal, held her breath, and watched.

Ned rose quickly from the shadows and moved to the office doorway. When Trisha saw him, she nearly jumped out of her seat.

"Who—who are you?" she gasped. "What do you want?"

"Never mind that," Ned said in his most threatening voice. "I know all about Dan. And the Denver connection."

"You—what? I don't know what you're talking about!" Ned's act was working, Nancy realized. Trisha was clearly thrown. Push her, Ned! Nancy urged him silently. Don't let her off the hook!

"I'm talking about a tall guy in a cowboy hat," Ned said almost as if he'd heard Nancy. "I know you're in on it together. I know about Dan's trips to Denver. I know about the envelope."

"How?" she challenged him. "How do you know?"

"I was a friend of Dan's. Call me his insurance policy. I know everything," he snapped, walking over to the desk.

Trisha's voice was husky with fear. "What do you want from me?"

Ned smiled, and sat down right on the desk.

Leaning over to Trisha, he purred, "I want in. You let me take Dan Taylor's place, and I keep what I know to myself."

There was silence as Trisha summed up the situation. The store manager was tough, Nancy thought. She wasn't quite ready to break.

"I—I still don't know what you're talking about," she insisted.

Time for the cavalry, Nancy thought. She gave Nikki a tap on the shoulder and nodded for her to join Ned.

Nancy shoved a carton onto the floor. It dropped with a thud.

"What was that?" Trisha gasped.

Ned feigned panic. "Who's out there?" he demanded in a shaky voice.

At that very moment, Nikki emerged from the shadows. "I've heard enough!" she shrieked, a realistic edge of insanity in her voice. It raised goosebumps on Nancy's arms. Nancy could only imagine the effect it had on Trisha Rapp.

"I know you killed Dan!" Nikki raved, pointing her finger at Ned's face. "You'll never get away with it! Never!"

Nikki pulled the starter's pistol out of her pocket and waved it in the air.

"No! No!" Ned shouted, as Nikki aimed the gun at his face. "It wasn't me! She did it!" he said, pointing at the stunned Trisha.

Nikki hesitated for a moment, as if wondering

145

whether or not to believe Ned. Then she leveled the pistol at Trisha.

"So you're in this, too!" she hissed.

Trisha backed up against the wall, terror reflected in her eyes.

"I loved Dan Taylor!" Nikki screamed. "Nobody cared about that. You just killed him in cold blood and left me behind to take the blame! Well, you won't get away with it. Let them put me away for a thousand years—I don't care!"

She cocked the gun and leveled it at Ned. He made as if to stop her, but before he could say anything, she fired. With a cry, Ned slumped to the ground and lay motionless. A pool of stage blood spread slowly on the ground around him.

Her eyes wild with triumph, Nikki turned back to Trisha and aimed the gun again.

That was enough for Trisha. "No! No, don't shoot!" she screamed. "Please, please don't kill me! I didn't kill him, I swear it."

Nikki's face took on a grim and determined expression. "You've got till the count of ten to tell me who did," she said somberly. "One. Two. Three—"

"It was Alan Harrow—one of our suppliers from Denver."

So that was his name, Nancy thought, the man in the cowboy hat.

Nancy stepped out from the shadows. "Nice

work, guys," she said as Ned got up from the floor and handed her the tape recorder.

Lifting up the phone, Nancy dialed police headquarters. "Hello, Chief McGinnis?" she said into the phone. "This is Nancy Drew. Meet me at Vanities right away. I think we've solved the Taylor murder."

Chapter

Seventeen

Dᴵᴰɴ'ᴛ I ᴛᴇʟʟ ʏᴏᴜ it was the guy in the cowboy hat?" Bess had her arm around Nancy's shoulder and was riding her mercilessly. It was the next day, and the Masters family was celebrating. A couple of Nikki's friends were there, too.

"Yes, Bess, you said it was him, all right," Nancy answered lightly. "But you also mentioned everyone else on my list. There was no way you could have been wrong."

Everyone laughed, except Bess. George laughed loudest of all. "She's right, Bess," she said apologetically.

"Seriously though, Bess," Nancy added, soothing her friend's ruffled feathers, "if you and

George hadn't gone to Vanities that day, I'd never have known about the Denver connection."

Nikki came over to them and held up a newspaper. The headline read: "Suspects Arrested in Taylor Murder."

"I'll be grateful to you for the rest of my life," said Nikki, giving Nancy a big hug. "But I'll never understand how you figured it out!"

Robin, seated on the couch next to Lacey, called out, "Me, neither. Like the watch. Nikki really was with Dan at ten-fourteen, wasn't she?"

"Nikki was with Dan at ten-fourteen, River Heights time, Robin. Dan's watch was set for Denver time," Nancy explained. "He must have forgotten to reset it when he got back into town."

"But how did the whole robbery scheme work, Nancy?" George asked. "I don't quite get it."

Nancy cleared her throat. "Trisha filled me in on that when she was arrested. According to her, she knew Alan Harrow from Denver. They'd been in on little scams before, but this one was their biggest caper yet.

"The idea was this: Trisha stole merchandise from Vanities and sent it to Denver via Dan Taylor. Al paid Dan off and resold the merchandise! Dan took Trisha's cut back to her, and the whole round would start over again."

"But if she was behind it, why did Trisha tell Kate Hayes about the thefts in the first place?" Bess asked, confused.

"I asked Kate about that when she came by the store before the police took Trisha off," Nancy said. "I thought it was strange, too. Apparently, Charlene was about to tell her, when Trisha overheard and pointed it out. I imagine she thought it would be embarrassing for her to be store manager and not know about it."

George shook her head. "It's all so weird. I mean, why take the dresses and all if she's making good money with the stolen jewelry? It seems to me that's where she went wrong."

"You're right, George," Ned said. "But by the end, there, I don't think Trisha was thinking too clearly. Maybe she just got greedy."

"Or maybe Mr. Cowboy Hat put her up to it," Bess suggested melodramatically.

The room was quiet. Then Nikki spoke up.

"But why did they have to kill Dan?" she asked, heartbroken.

"Trisha knew if Dan accused her of anything, she could point to his reputation as a liar. But she didn't figure on Dan having enough brains to take out 'insurance.' He'd been saving tags, duplicate invoices, anything he could get his hands on."

"It says here," said Nikki, pointing to the paper, "that they found the envelope in Harrow's condo."

Nancy shook her head. "I guess he decided to keep it as insurance against Trisha. Anyway, when Dan told them he was quitting, they got worried that he was going to go to the police. That's why Alan Harrow was in town: to shut Dan up. I think Dan knew that. And that's why he tried to give Nikki the envelope."

"I can't help thinking I let Dan down," Nikki said softly. "Just when he needed me most, too."

Nancy put an arm around her neighbor's slender shoulders. "Nikki, you did the right thing, given what you knew. Besides, you might have wound up just like Dan."

Nikki shuddered. "Sometimes I wonder if I'll ever get over this," she said.

"Of course you will," Nancy told her. "Sooner than you think."

She motioned for Ned, Bess, and George to follow her outside. It was time for Nikki to get back to her family and friends—to her real, everyday world.

Outside, it was another perfect late-summer afternoon. "Hey, nice new window, Drew!" Bess laughed as they crossed the lawn. "Who was responsible for that little stunt, by the way?"

"Trisha," answered Nancy matter-of-factly. "She told me in the back of the squad car on the way to the station. She actually seemed sorry about it," she mused. "Apparently, Harrow freaked when Trisha told him I was on the case and made her do it. After you," she gestured, allowing Bess and George to go inside.

Before she could follow them in, Ned pulled her aside and put a small box in her hand. "I didn't get a chance to give you this yesterday," he apologized. Opening the box, Nancy removed an elegant gold bracelet.

"Happy anniversary, Nan," Ned said.

Nancy looked up, misty eyed. "Thanks for being my boyfriend, Ned Nickerson," she said softly. "You're the greatest."

"You're not half bad yourself," he murmured softly, kissing her.

Standing on the front porch, the two of them turned around to look out at the street.

"You know," Nancy told him, resting her head on his shoulder. "I mistrusted Trisha Rapp the first time I met her."

"Oh?" Ned said casually. "And why was that?"

"She didn't think much of River Heights!" Nancy exclaimed. "Can you imagine any decent person not liking River Heights?"